DYRE

A KNIGHT OF SPIRIT AND SHADOWS

By the Author

Dyre: By Moon's Light

Visit us at www.boldstrokesbooks.com

DYRE
A KNIGHT OF SPIRIT AND SHADOWS

by

Rachel E. Bailey

2016

DYRE: A KNIGHT OF SPIRIT AND SHADOWS
© 2016 BY RACHEL E. BAILEY. ALL RIGHTS RESERVED.

ISBN 13: 978-1-62639-664-7

THIS TRADE PAPERBACK ORIGINAL IS PUBLISHED BY
BOLD STROKES BOOKS, INC.
P.O. BOX 249
VALLEY FALLS, NY 12185

FIRST EDITION: AUGUST 2016

CREDITS
EDITOR: JERRY L. WHEELER
PRODUCTION DESIGN: STACIA SEAMAN
COVER DESIGN BY JEANINE HENNING

Acknowledgments

For everyone who wouldn't let me skive off this second novel.

For everyone who asked how the novel was coming along at every stage of it.

For everyone who told me: "Keep going."

Well…I kept going. Thanks.

To my mother. Thanks for putting up with my descent into antisocial angst while I wrote this.

PROLOGUE

Ever has it been that love knows not its own depth until the hour of separation.

—Khalil Gibran

There was darkness and nothingness—a horrible place in which Ruby felt trapped, unable to do anything but mark the sluggish passage of time. A place where even the silver light of the Untamed could not penetrate.

Then there was light. Sunlight shining through her eyelids, warm and cheerful, running over her skin like honey. She stretched her slightly stiff limbs and opened her eyes slowly. Yellow light prized its way through her shuttered lashes and she hissed, blinking impatiently to get used to the sunshine.

When she could see well enough to look around, she found herself in an unfamiliar bedroom.

It was enormous, decorated like the kind of luxury hotel room Ruby could never have afforded to stay in, once upon a time. Done in cream, tan, and mahogany, with low, understated furniture that looked expensive, it had large picture windows and a balcony with glass doors that stood open, letting in a warm, gentle breeze that blew back linen curtains. Post-colonial art adorned the walls and complemented the décor.

The room had three doors, all of them closed. In the midst

of this opulence, Ruby lay ensconced in a huge bed, as naked as the day she was born.

Struggling in the scads of white pillows, she sat up and swung her legs over the side of the bed. She expected to feel dizzy or nauseous or disoriented, considering her last memories of being drugged, but she felt mostly fine. A little stiff, a little iffy—and with a definite case of cottonmouth—but fine.

She stood up carefully, levering herself out of the soft clutches of the bed, and made her way to the nearest door, the wood of the floor warm under her feet. She turned the knob, and the door swung open easily enough, revealing a closet filled with sundresses. Frowning, she closed the door again, quietly, and tried the door across from the balcony.

It opened on a lavish bathroom. Ruby suddenly felt the urgent call of nature and made use of this discovery. She washed her hands, splashed water on her face, and looked in the mirror. She looked the same as ever, though a bit more peaked and pale under her complexion. Her hair was an absolute mess that would no doubt take hours to fix. Turning away from her reflection, she exited the bathroom and tried the third door.

The knob turned, but the door was locked from the outside.

Not terribly surprised, Ruby let go of the knob and went to the balcony. Even a quick glance showed she couldn't escape that way, for the balcony overlooked a sheer drop into the bluest sea Ruby had ever seen. What seemed like acres across the water were rocky cliffs that also sported balconies interspersed throughout their faces. To the east, the cliffs let out to the open sea. To the west, Ruby's cliff face eventually curved around to form the cliff face across from her, like a stubby letter *U*.

"Well, even assuming I survived the dive, I can't fucking *swim* and haven't got anywhere to swim *to*," she muttered ruefully. And, silently, *Plus, I'm not going anywhere without Des.*

Which was working on the assumption that Des was still alive, wherever she was. The only thing keeping her relatively calm at this moment was assuming Des was maybe even back at Coulter Manor, working with Thierry to find her.

Turning back into the room, Ruby closed the doors behind her, trying her best not to cry. If nothing else, Des would find her. And when she did…when she did…

Ruby wrapped her arms around herself and imagined those arms were Des's. Imagined them tightening and never letting go again. She imagined Des's low, raspy, smart-ass voice telling her that everything was okay. Of course it was okay. Des had it under control. It may not look like it from certain angles, but everything was totally copacetic. Five by five.

Laughing a little waterlogged giggle, Ruby squeezed herself tight for a moment then let go, brushing her hair back out of her face and tugging on it a little. Whatever else happened, Des would find her, and together, they'd go back home. Ruby knew it in her bones. Knew it down at a sub-atomic level. It was just a matter of time. Never mind that Ruby didn't know what her captors wanted and didn't know how much time she had before they got desperate.

Never mind that.

Des would find her.

Taking a whiff of herself, Ruby decided that in the meantime, the first thing she required of her sumptuous prison was a shower. At the very least, she could be clean and dressed—assuming any of the clothes in that closet fit—for whenever her kidnappers decided to make an appearance. Being clean and dressed might not level the playing field much, but it would make her feel better. It wasn't much of a game plan, but it was the best she could do on short notice.

And until her captors put in an appearance, it was really the *only* thing she could do.

Part I: City of Lights

When there is no sun or moon for guidance, look to the stars.
—Karon Yoo

CHAPTER ONE

One moment, Des was so deeply asleep, it was as if she'd stopped existing. The next, she bolted upright in her own bed, screaming, "No!"

"Easy there, slugger, you're all right," Jake said from her bedside, not flinching away when she whirled to face him, eyes wide, teeth bared.

"They took her!" she exclaimed, fists clenched so tightly blood began to issue from them. She barely noticed the sting of her punctured palms. "They *took* her!"

Jake nodded grimly.

"Well, what're we doing to get her back?" Des demanded, throwing aside the coverlet and jumping up so fast she got dizzy and reeled a little. Jake caught her easily and pushed her back down to the bed.

"Thierry's people are on it—"

"What does that even mean? Do they have any leads? Did they find out *who* took her?"

Jake sat back in his chair, looking pale and haggard. "There was nothing to find out. They didn't try to hide the fact that it was them."

"Who, Jake?" Des leaned forward on the edge of her bed. "If we know who, we can make them bleed until we get her back!"

"It's not that easy, Des—"

"Yes, it is. Tell me who has her, and if you don't wanna get your hands dirty, I damn sure will."

"Des—" Jake pleaded, and Des recognized the plea for what it was. He was asking her to be patient and reasonable. But Des was so far beyond either patience or reason, under any other circumstances Jake's pleas would've been laughable.

"Jacob."

They both looked around. James closed the door to Des's room and leaned against it wearily. For once, he looked as done in and harried as his lover.

"Tell her, Jake. She has every right to know. It's not like it's a secret," he said gravely.

Jake looked away from them for a few moments. Des felt the time passing. They could be getting Ruby back. She wanted to grind her teeth in frustration, to grab her brother and shake the answers she needed out of him. But he spoke before she lost the self-control she had left.

"It was Evelyn and Julian." Jake shook his head. "We don't know how they got her off the property yet, but they're the ones who've got her. Or had her."

Des blinked. Having only seen the pair from a distance, she couldn't say one way or the other whether she would've put this past them. As to their motives, who knew? "Why?" she asked James, who shrugged.

"I don't know. All I know is, Julian was the mastermind of this little abduction. My sister would *never* have come up with this on her—"

"Save it," Des said flatly, standing carefully this time. "Do we think they were involved with the incident at Lenape Hall?"

Neither man answered, which was all the answer Des needed. "Right. Do we have any idea where they could have taken her?"

"Thierry was able to track their movements to the airport. Julian's jet was scheduled to make a one-way trip to Paris. From there, they seem to have disappeared off the face of the Earth."

Jake spread his hands then ran them through his hair. "We just keep losing people, damnit!"

"Not her. Not her," Des said, stalking to her closet. She threw on whatever came to hand then faced her brother, who'd been joined by a worried James. "Where's LaFours now?"

"Paris. Where else?" James took Jake's hand and kissed it gently. "Shall we schedule you a flight?"

"Please do." Des was already digging her duffel out of the back of her closet.

❖

The clothes fit so well, Ruby began to wonder if she'd been measured in her sleep. She hastily pushed that creepy thought out of her mind and settled on the least frilly outfit to be had, a simple white sundress with red flowers at the waist in lieu of a belt, and a pair of comfortable gold sandals. It wasn't her style, really, but it was better than greeting her captors in the buff.

So, clean and dressed, she made her way to a chaise near the balcony doors and sat. And watched. And waited for the knob of the locked door to turn.

She didn't have to wait long. Within minutes, the doorknob turned and clicked, and the door opened.

"*Evelyn?*" Ruby shook her head, certain she was seeing things. But the elegantly dressed woman in the doorway didn't so much as waver. Instead, she smiled a cool, otherwise unreadable smile and stepped into the bedroom, shutting the door.

"I see the clothes fit," she said, apropos of absolutely nothing.

Ruby's mouth dropped open, and she stammered for most of a minute before something coherent came out. "Where am I? What's going on? Is Des okay?"

Evelyn's cool smile turned almost chagrined, as if she had been expecting some other reaction than sheer confusion. "You're at a Den in the Mediterranean. Your *Geas*-protector is fine, last

I checked—she's back at Coulter Manor, in the States. As to what's going on—" Evelyn crossed the spacious room till she was a mere few feet away. "The situation is rather complicated, and will take some time to explain. Suffice it to say it's urgent you be made aware of the particulars and your options, and that we have your full cooperation in settling things before next Full Moon."

Ruby frowned, shaking her head. "'We' being who? Besides the people who kidnapped me from my home, that is?"

Evelyn twitched a little, almost a wince. "We are certain factions of the European Council of Alphas, which is modeled closely on the North American Council. And I apologize on their behalf for the rather desperate measure we resorted to, to obtain your ear and your cooperation. But it had to be done. We had no time for the niceties of diplomacy."

"And why is that?" Ruby asked calmly, though she was shaking and cold inside. "What was so urgent that you saw the need to kidnap me rather than ask me if I wouldn't mind helping?"

Evelyn sighed and began to pace. "What if I told you it was a matter of the lives and deaths of thousands of Loups? That the situation the European Packs are facing is civil war, which will inevitably spread to the Americas?"

Ruby's mouth dropped open then snapped shut. The shakes grew more pronounced. "I'd say that's a terrible fix to be in, but that I didn't see how European civil unrest has anything to do with the American Packs."

Evelyn conceded this point gracefully. "It has to do, actually, with Father and his meddling into Pack affairs and with traditions. Unfortunately—" Here, Evelyn swallowed, her lips pursing and nostrils flaring. "Unfortunately for him, his involvement with certain factions opposing ours resulted in his death."

"You know who killed George? And it's the same people who're pulling your strings now?" Ruby demanded, horrified.

Evelyn colored but held her head high. "As I said, the

situation is complicated. Factions that would see Packs revert to the Old Ways are on the rise in Europe. They'd like to see the Councils of Alphas disbanded and the equivalent of feudal states set up in their place. Rights and privileges would no longer be voted and compromised on, but fought over, and the title of Alpha would be hereditary—contestable only through combat. Father was, of course, against such a thing. His thinking, I believe, was that this ideology would spread from Europe to the North American Packs—"

"In which case, you'd be in my place right now," Ruby interrupted. Evelyn twitched again. "I take it you disagreed with George's views on Loup politics. You're for these Reversionists?"

"'Reversionists'?" Evelyn smiled again, wryly. "I suppose that's as good a name for us as any. And yes, I'm a Reversionist. Democracy is a fine idea for Humes. But for Loups, I believe the Old Ways are best.

"Some of us, however, as with many, take our zeal a step too far. One of the more rabid, for lack of a better word, Reversionist factions was responsible for the death of my father and for the attack on Coulter Manor."

Stunned and speechless, Ruby could only gape before her eyes filled with tears. "And you're still siding with them? They killed your father!"

"I'm not siding with anyone, I'm supporting an ideology. And the rabid factions among the Reversionists are being carefully rooted out and contained. Or destroyed." Evelyn crossed her arms and rocked back on her heels. "We're at great pains to remedy the situation. The whole situation. Which is why we need you."

"Need me to what?"

Gazing at Ruby as if measuring her, Evelyn finally closed the distance between them and sat down on the chaise. "I—we—need you to support our aims in the coming months. We need as many Loups, no matter where they're from, to come down on the side of a set of traditions that's as old as Loups themselves," she said plainly, her blue-blue eyes steady on Ruby's. "DyreMother, we need your blessing and the backing of the North American Garoul to quash this impending civil war."

"That's—I'm barely a Loup myself! I just had my first Change the night before you guys kidnapped me!" Ruby shook her head. "I don't have the sway among the North American Garoul you seem to think I have."

Evelyn seemed amused at this statement. "That's where you're wrong, Ruby. No matter who you were, or who you think you are, you're the DyreMother now. Your Packs would fight for you, die for you, and follow you to the ends of the Earth. The Old Ways speak to Loups in our blood and bones. In our spirits. We've let ourselves be tamed because the times seemed to demand it, but we should have been standing up for our rights to be who and what we are."

Ruby looked down at her feet. "That's not what George thought, was it? He believed the Garoul should change with the times. Evolve and progress. Grow up." She sensed rather than saw Evelyn sit back a little. "Knowing when to break with tradition is the foundation of the North American Packs, isn't it? That's a large part of why Callum Coulter came to North America in the first place. He wanted to found his own Pack where leadership and privilege was based on merit and democracy, rather than tradition and primogeniture."

Evelyn was silent for a minute, clearly thinking this over. Ruby didn't dare look at her. She didn't know where the words had come from, but they felt right. In her bones and blood and spirit, they felt right. They felt like something of which George might have approved.

"You haven't been Loup long enough to understand the importance of Garoul tradition, Ruby," Evelyn began kindly but rather condescendingly.

"But I've been Loup long enough to support something I completely disagree with? And take my Packs with me?" Ruby snorted. "You can't have it both ways. I'm either Loup enough or I'm not. And since you've gone to all the trouble of kidnapping me and stashing me here, I'd say I'm Loup enough."

"Perhaps. But that doesn't mean you know all there is to know about life as one of the Garoul."

"But I know what George and all the North American Dyres before him knew. Or I will, won't I?" Ruby looked over at Evelyn, who was frowning. "Granted, I don't remember yet, but every new thing I learn about the Garoul is familiar to me. As if I'm being reminded of something I already know. Even your spiel about tradition and the Old Ways feels like something I've heard before. And that's because part of me has, hasn't it?"

Evelyn narrowed her eyes and deepened her frown. "You mean the passing of knowledge and memory with the Death-right?" She waved a hand dismissively. "That phenomenon has never been properly documented in Garoul history, despite what the Coulters may have told you."

"I trust them and your brother more than I trust you and the people you're working for," Ruby said quietly as Evelyn sat back again. "I'm not usually one to follow my gut, but in this case, I think it's right on the money. So's George's Death-right. Not a single one of the Dyres who preceded me would have supported your ideology, and neither can I."

"Not even if it meant getting your life back?"

Now Ruby was the one to frown, and Evelyn's smile reappeared like the sun from behind storm clouds.

"How would you like to be able to go back to your old life? One that's free of the responsibilities of being the Dyre, free of the politics and the terrible onus of leading tens of thousands of Loups." Evelyn's perfectly sculpted blond brows quirked above her nakedly triumphant eyes. "How would you like to have an entirely new life? To be able to travel, see the world, live comfortably, do whatever it is you want to do with your life, and only have to worry about being a Loup once a month?"

Ruby blinked in surprise, and a tear ran down her face. "That's not possible."

"Supposing it is. Would that appeal to you?"

Ruby took a breath and looked over her shoulder out the balcony door. The view was spectacular, despite the circumstances. "I didn't ask for this. Any of it. But there's nothing I can do to change it. George passed his Death-right on to me. The only way I can get out of being the Dyre is dying."

"What if there was another way?"

"There isn't another way."

"But what if there was?"

Turning away from the view, Ruby looked down at her hands. She thought about Jake and James, Nathan and Philomena. She thought of Thierry and of Des, and all the Loups she'd met since waking up at Coulter Manor. She thought of them and how she'd been fooling herself thinking she could ever properly lead them, even with the leeway of time to study and prepare. Since the Purge, Jake and James had been doing the leading, both of the Coulter Pack and the Packs in general, while new Alphas contested and maneuvered their ways into power.

They had been doing Ruby's job, holding the Packs together until things were settled once more. Under the guise of observation and learning, Ruby had been hiding from what was, ultimately, her responsibility and no one else's.

Had George chosen the best candidate for the job of Dyre or had he simply made the only choice available to him at the moment of his death? Wouldn't almost anybody be a better leader than someone who didn't want the job and who deep down knew she couldn't do it, Death-right or not?

More tears rolled down Ruby's face and she wiped them away irritably. She opened her mouth to tell Evelyn that she wasn't for sale, no matter the price. But what came out instead was:

"I'm listening."

❖

"Jenn, honey, you're gonna be late!"
Des opened her eyes and bolted upright, still caught in the vestiges of the weirdest dream. She shook her head groggily and swung her legs over the side of her bed, barely noting the coverlet and sheet she'd tossed aside. She felt disoriented and almost faint.

"Coming, Ma!" she called, clearing her throat. Then she was shaking her head again at the sensation of offness—of wrongness—that persisted even as she got up and, forsaking a shower, got dressed.

She slung on her backpack automatically when she was done, her books still in there exactly as they had been when she'd left school the day before. Homework was for losers, and Des's spiraling grades could attest she was anything but a loser. As she was leaving, she looked around her tornado alley of a room. Everything was in its place, or at least where she'd left it lying. Her mother rarely bothered to clean Des's room anymore. She knew it was a thankless, hopeless task.

Not finding anything physically out of place in her room, Des turned to go, brow furrowed, frowning.

This is all wrong, she thought, and she tried to remember the dream she'd had last night. Sometimes, just sometimes, she'd had dreams that left this sort of strangeness in their wake. Dreams she barely remembered, but that sometimes came true, said events leaving behind a sense of deja vu so strong, it left Des breathless. But always after the dreams, she had a sense of something having changed about her reality. A sense of difference, if not outright wrongness.

But this dream had left definite wrongness in its wake, and for the life of her, Des couldn't remember what it'd been about, only that it had been long and strange and sad.

When she got to the kitchen, her mother was at the stove, smoking, and frying sausages and eggs. The sausage and eggs smelled good. The cigarette smoke did not. It nearly made Des retch. It did that a lot lately. Many things did, as if Des's sense of smell was on overdrive. Certain scents, even good scents, had a way of intensifying to the point of being unbearable.

Her mother's cigarettes, never the best of scents but familiar and comforting, made her stomach turn over and her eyeballs throb.

"P-U! Someone put out the fire," she said, sliding into her usual chair at the kitchen table and dropping her backpack on the floor with a heavy chunk*. From her post at the stove, her mother snorted.*

"Trust me, Jenny, you'd like your old ma a lot less without her morning cigarette," she muttered around her cancer stick. "Forget to set your alarm clock last night?"

Des shook her head again, thinking wrong-wrong-wrong*. "Musta slept right through it, I guess. I'm pretty sure I set it."*

"Hmm. Maybe you need to go to sleep earlier."

"I fell asleep before ten last night!"

"And obviously eight hours wasn't enough."

"Only sick people sleep for longer than eight hours. Or, like, coal miners. I'm usually good with five or six, you know that." Des tried on a smile as her mother faced her holding a plate with breakfast. Her mother smiled, too, a smile that was still pretty despite the lines that bracketed it. But it was a fragile smile, as if she knew deep down maybe she'd better get all her smiling in now, before it was too late.

Des frowned at the unfamiliar, rather unpleasant thought then dismissed it, taking her plate. She immediately began to wolf down the sausage. It was crispy on the outside, sizzling and greasy on the inside.

"It's a good thing I'm not a vegetarian, or you'd be up the creek," Ma said, amusement coloring her voice. "Honestly, I've never seen anyone tear into dead animal flesh like you."

I must get it from my father, Des thought, but didn't say. She'd learned early on not to bring up the mysterious Father-Person who'd vanished like so much smoke from their lives before Des was even born. "I'm a growing girl. I need my daily requirements of protein, iron, and mesquite."

Des's mother snorted again. "Don't leave the eggs to go to waste."

"I won't." Des was, in fact, already hoovering up her eggs. They were good, as always, but nothing could quite touch the taste of meat. Any kind of meat. "I'm hungry."

"You're always hungry." Her mother laughed and sat at the table, smoking as she watched Des eat. This wasn't unusual, but it made Des's hackles raise for some reason this particular morning.

Eggs finally done, sausage a mere memory, Des finally looked up into her mother's eyes. They weren't their usual kind, medium brown, but a keen, eldritch green not at all at home in her mother's pretty, tired face. This should have been startling, but it wasn't. That sense of wrongness finally dissipated some, as if pieces of the puzzle were starting to rearrange themselves into positions that made sense.

Who or whatever was sitting across from Des was not her mother. It was as simple as that. It couldn't be her mother. For one thing, it smelled of nothing at all, and her mother always smelled like perfume or paper or makeup, new smoke, old smoke, something Des could always sniff out of a crowd of scents and identify.

And for another thing, her mother was dead. Long dead.

Des picked up her fork again and, heeding nothing more than her instinct, threw it up into the air, where it stayed as if held by an invisible force. After a minute of staring at it and waiting for gravity to kick in, but not actually willing the fork to come clattering down to the table, Des looked at the person sitting across from her, noting the slightly lengthened features and the canny grin.

"Either I'm asleep or we're in the Matrix," Des said calmly. The person across from her laughed, sitting back in the chair and crossing one still-shapely leg over the other. She adjusted Des's mother's skirt so that it covered her knees.

"Couldn't it be both?" the woman said glibly, still in her mother's voice. "Ruby used to try to get George to watch The Matrix, *but she occasionally displayed such a deplorable taste in films, he never did give it a try. He always took her movie recommendations with a grain of salt."*

The name Ruby *struck a bell in Des's mind, and she sat up, rod-straight. The last, lingering sense of wrongness settled into a feeling of grim realization, failure, and shame.*

"Oh, Moon Above," she moaned, burying her face in her hands, hot tears slipping through her fingers as knowledge and remembrance danced in her foggy brain. "I fucked up. I fucked up so bad."

"Oh, no doubt about it," the other agreed chummily. "But you're young. It's to be expected. Usually Geas-*protectors are some decades older when they get sworn. There's greater life experience to inform them when they're called. Not to mention they've usually never been rabid, either."*

Des sniffed and wiped at her face, but her tears still fell. "Yeah, well. I can't blame all my failures on having once been rabid. That was almost four years ago!"

"A veritable lifetime," the other noted, and Des laughed ruefully.

"I was rabid. Took lives. Got a second chance. Got better.

Took the oath. Failed. Took the oath again, and failed Ruby, too."
Des ran her fingers up into her spiky bed-head hair and tugged.
"Everything I touch turns to shit."

*"Oh, stop feeling sorry for yourself. It won't solve anything,
and it just wastes the precious time we've got here."*

Stung but chastened, Des wiped at her face again and looked
the other in her eerie green eyes. *"Where's here and who are
you?"*

The other smiled, almost kindly. *"Here is of no import. And
I am just another humble part of the Untamed. I'm the deus
ex machina of the novel that is your life. The Ghost of* Geas-
Protectors *Past, kid. Only I'm not here to show you the mistakes
you've made. You can already see those for yourself. I'm here to
show you something a lot more useful."*

"Useful?" Des asked, still trying to process the rest of what
the other had said.

"That's right. There're a few tricks of the Geas-protector
*trade no one let you in on when you were sworn into office.
Deliberately, I might add."* A baleful flash in those creepy green
eyes made Des sit back, shuddering. And the other's voice, she
noticed, no longer sounded like her mother at all. It was rather
androgynous, with a faint accent too light and lost in her quick
patter for Des to place it. *"You might want to look into that
sometime soon. Someone who had a hand in choosing you did
so with the intention of you failing your Dyre. Which isn't to say
George's death isn't a burden you must bear, but it's a burden
of which you can relieve yourself by half. You were chosen for
your youth, your vulnerability, and your ignorance. You were
untrained, uninformed, and unready. You're still not ready, but
that's become irrelevant. Your Dyre needs you, and you're the
only one who can save her."*

"But how?" Des shrugged helplessly. *"Follow my fucking
nose?"*

That canny grin became a little uncanny. *"Metaphorically*

speaking, yes. And I can show you how." She stood up and circled around to where Des was sitting. It looked less like her mother and more like a stranger now. Taller, leaner, with lighter hair, darker skin, and the faint markings of old scars on its face and hands.

"Get ready," it said, kneeling in front of Des and leaning so close, Des could see flecks of gray in the green of its eyes.

"Ready for what?" Des swallowed and tried not to pull away as the other took her hands and squeezed them. Its own hands were cold and dry, like ancient marble.

"To learn some badass, nth-level Jedi shit, young Padawan." It laughed like a dog yipping and then it clasped Des's head, one hand on her forehead, the other on her crown. "Hold on, this might sting a bit."

"What might sting a—oooOOOOOO!" Des howled and writhed in the chair as what felt like every cell of her brain was blasted with bright, burning silver light.

"Feel that?" it asked through what sounded like gritted teeth. "That's just a small percentage of the unused portion of your brain being lit up by electrons and neurons and shit. And off topic? Lemme tell you, you've got one stubborn brain. It doesn't take kindly to intruders, no matter how many gifts they bear. But the Untamed Heart is stubborner."

Des didn't doubt it. She slid out of her chair to the floor in a limp puddle of Loup. She felt her brain being shut down, and the other, the Ghost of Geas-Protectors Past, no longer looked like her mother. It looked vaguely like Thierry LaFours, neither short nor tall, wiry, but strong and sharp of feature, with a sensual mouth that implied brooding more than it did anything else.

Alarmed, Des tried to flap the other's hands away from her head, but it held on tight.

"Sorry, kid. Almost done, but I gotta make sure it is done. There's no room for almost-did in this game," the other said, its eyes squinched shut with concentration. "Gotta make sure you

can do what needs to be done, and no more of this you versus the Loup dichotomy. You are the Loup, Des, and it's time you two were made one."

That silver-light-burn intensified, and Des continued to howl. She felt as if that light was rifling through every fiber of her being, looking for something, changing everything it touched in its search, including Des herself.

"Damn, kid. Your sixth sense's really playing hide 'n' seek," the other said through still-gritted teeth. "But don't you worry, we'll get you tricked out in no time."

"Let. Go. Of. Me!" Des panted out as those burning silver fingers suddenly stopped flipping through the pages of her mind.

THERE, came a voice from her mind, but not of it. It was the strangest sensation Des ever hoped to feel. Her body went limp, sprawling on the kitchen floor, twitching and shaking, though the other gently lowered her head to the linoleum and finally released its grip on Des's skull.

"See? Told ya we'd find it. And soon you'll be all set," it crooned gently, hesitating before smiling. "For what it's worth, I'm sorry it had to be this way. If everything had been done aboveboard, this knowledge and power would've come to you slowly, naturally, over time. Unfortunately, time is a luxury you don't have anymore."

It stood up and stretched, now a lean, male figure in Des's mother's housedress. After stretching, it watched Des twitch and shake with a dissatisfied expression on its long face.

"I'm sorry," it said again, then shrugged. "But trust me on this, if nothing else. You'll be glad of the power when it kicks in. Maybe not so much right away. Even short-range telepathy is never a plus in an airport, especially Charles de Gaulle, but afterward...yeah. Oh! And if you don't mind doing me a tiny favor, when you see them, tell Thierry and Nicolae that Philippe says 'salut' for me, would you?"

What? Des thought just as the other vanished, without so

much as a puff of smoke. Pressure gathered inside her skull and began to increase, like someone pressing a finger onto her brain and pushing inward with no small amount of force. It didn't hurt, but the feeling wasn't pleasant, either. She fought it as hard as she could, as best she could, but it was like fighting a thousand enemies. The pressure seemed to be coming from all directions, and no matter how fast she mentally kung-fu'd, she couldn't block them for longer than it took for them to come from another direction.

Worst of all, she got the distinct impression that the pressure was playing with her. Feinting and testing her, to see what she was made of.

Suddenly incensed, Des tried her best to calm herself down and slow the beehive of light-speed thoughts. She stopped her mental kung-fu and let the pressure in her mind build and build, parry and poke. Meanwhile, she was imagining her mind as water, movable, containable, but not attainable. Easy to shift but impossible to grab.

That sense of pressure immediately lifted and was gone. Her mind had been, briefly, turned off—no, restarted and rebooted with a completely different operating system. Des 2.0. She could smell sounds, taste colors, feel scents. She could see through the lids of her closed eyes, see the kitchen of the house she'd grown up in, only it wasn't really. Behind and beyond that was nothing but silver light that smelled of the wind and trees and grass, of other predators and even of prey. But beyond that was—

Pain, as sharp as it was sudden, ripped into Des's skull as she squinted this new, sixth sense at the silver light and whatever was beyond it. Her sight collapsed in on itself and she collapsed to the thankfully solid, though no less imaginary linoleum floor.

Left side of her head pounding like the worst migraine ever, she rolled onto her mostly numb left side and curled into fetal position, shaking and barely able to see past her own nose. That doubled drip-splat sound she heard coming from her left nostril and her left ear, respectively, smelled like her own blood. Closing her eyes on the fake world, Des let go of consciousness, sinking into darkness as soft as it was deep, and as silent as it was eternal. Well, silent and eternal, until...

"Ladies and gentleman, please return your seats to their upright positions. We're approaching Charles de Gaulle Airport—"

❖

"—and will be landing shortly." A soft, accented voice pierced the darkness. Groaning, she tried to hide from the voice, to bury herself in the restful dark. But the *real* waking world wasn't about to be denied. It came bearing the outliers of a monstrous headache and pervasive soreness that made holding on to the protective darkness all but impossible.

As it slipped away, light naturally took its place, and with light came the memory of a bright, silvery curtain she'd dared to try and see beyond.

No! Not again—next time, it'll kill me—

Des gasped and bolted upright, blinking groggily as she found herself in a seat in the first class cabin of a commercial airliner. She looked at the people closing overhead compartments and returning from the head to take their seats once more. Lifting a hand that seemed to weigh ten thousand pounds, Des rubbed her eyes and tried to sit up. A wave of nausea swept over her. She tasted salty, coppery blood and nearly gagged. Groaning, she let her body bear her forward, till she was leaning on the seat in front of her. That taste of blood intensified, and she realized she had a nosebleed. That went perfectly with the weird headache she had, at least on the left side of her head. The right side, though no great shakes at the moment, was relatively fine.

Blood was beginning to drip on the leg of her jeans.

"Mademoiselle? I'm afraid we have to ask you to buckle

your safety belt. We're about to land," a professionally kind voice said from Des's right. Groaning again, she levered herself upright and leaned back, rolling her eyes toward the voice. The pretty, older flight attendant looked quite startled when she saw Des. "You're bleeding!"

Des winced and glanced around to make sure the flight attendant's squeak hadn't drawn attention. "Just a nosebleed—I get 'em all the time," Des lied, smiling, hoping she didn't have blood in her teeth. From the newly startled look on the flight attendant's heart-shaped face, she probably did.

The attendant soon composed herself and produced a small packet of tissues from some unseen pocket. With mumbled thanks, Des tore into the packet and jammed the first tissue up her nose. "Thank you," she said again, trying another smile. This time, the flight attendant returned it and cleared her throat.

"Your ear—" she began, gesturing at Des's left ear. Des blanched. She pulled out another tissue and swiped quickly at her ear. Sure enough, the tissue came away bloody. And not a little.

"Crap!" Des blotted and blotted, swiped and wiped until she could be reasonably certain she'd gotten as much as she was going to get without water and a mirror, all under the flight attendant's professionally worried gaze.

"Uh, it's just an earbleed. I get those all the time, too," Des said, balling the tissue up and jamming it in her jacket pocket. She hastily buckled up and gave the flight attendant another grisly smile.

When she finally moved on, presumably to leave Des to her own bloody devices, Des let out a sigh and leaned her head back. She closed her exhausted eyes, and she could see the kitchen of her mother's house. Behind that shone silver light.

Behind the silver light… Des shivered, opening her eyes and withdrawing from the memory. *Curiosity may not have killed* this *cat, but it damn sure gave it a stroke or something. Holy* shit, she thought numbly. *Holy shit.*

So I'm apparently operating under the idea that that screwy dream was somehow real. At least what happened at the end happened in waking life. The rest of it may have been bullshit, but the ending...the bleeding was real. Or maybe I started bleeding before it happened in the dream, and my subconscious somehow incorporated it into the dream, and—

"Bullshit, eh?"

The voice was so close, so distinct, that Des thought it was the Loup. But it wasn't. In fact, she hadn't heard that separate yet distinct voice since she'd woken up. But who? She looked around for the speaker before she realized the voice, though separate from her, was still coming from inside her own head. It was the voice of the stranger in her dream that she'd first taken to be her mother.

Philippe.

"If you think what I told you was bullshit, just wait until you step out into Charles de Gaulle," Philippe, continued, sounding annoyed and smug and still, apparently, coming from inside Des's throbbing skull. "I don't envy you, kid. Just try and remember that little trick you came up with. They're wind, and you're water. They can move you, but they can't hold you. Good luck."

And just like that, it was gone, as suddenly as if her ears had popped, leaving Des alone but for a cabin full of people and the keen suspicion that she was going quietly insane.

❖

Despite her continued belief that at least part of the dream was bullshit, Des stepped into Charles de Gaulle warily, darting her eyes everywhere as if expecting an attack.

Nothing.

Nothing but a lot of tourists and business people, all scrambling and shuffling around for luggage and the correct gates for their connecting flights. Des's hackles and senses were cranked up all through Customs and Luggage Claim, waiting for something—*anything*—to happen.

Nothing.

Once she was through the rigmarole of getting herself out of the airport, duffel on shoulder, the first feelings hit her like a tsunami of confusion. One moment she was stumping along, not making any eye contact. Then someone bumped into her and was immediately, distractedly apologizing. But before they moved on, Des met irritated, indeed, distracted dark eyes. In a painful, purely mental flash of silver, for the second time in waking life that day, alien emotion filled her consciousness, carried on the backs of conversations. Annoyance-anger-resignation:

"—spend one more fucking moment in the middle of Charles-damned-de Gaulle waiting for her to find a crapper so she can reapply, I'm going to commit hara-kiri with my own damned pen—"

Then Des was shaking her head once hard, instinctively breaking eye contact, only to find herself looking up into someone else's absent gray-blue eyes. They belonged to a young man talking on his cell phone. She was almost swept away by sneakiness-smugness-arrogance.

"—je ne peux pas croire qu'elle me croit—maintenant, que dois-je dire à propos de Vanessa vendredi? Elle sait toujours quand je suis couché...Peut-être si je mélange un peu de la vérité—"

Then he glanced away at something or someone else, and Des was free of any emotions not her own. For a few moments, she was left standing utterly still in a sea of moving people, gobsmacked and almost dizzy, her duffel half hanging off her shoulder. Blood slowly began to trickle and drip from her nose, and as passersby started to notice, she didn't have to work to avoid eye contact anymore.

Des whined high and soft in the back of her throat, and she

staggered on through the parting crowd of tourists and commuters, squinting just enough to see where she was going. And it worked until the airport began to slowly, but surely spin.

"Uhhh," she groaned, one hand going up to a head that suddenly felt both too large and too small. Her hand was clammy and shaking, and her head was damp and slightly too warm. She glanced carefully around the revolving airport until she saw a row of empty seats in a waiting area. Reshouldering her duffel and taking a breath, she started toward the row of silvery seats when a whole wave of utterly unfamiliar emotions hit her. They began to buffet her like gale-force winds: overlaying all, annoyance in shades of tired, faded yellow at having to go through the banal horrors of any airport. Under that yellow layer of irritation, she felt emotions from arterial red rage to blue shades of anticipation.

She also saw the silken, sad, uncertain rustling of purple-tinted misery and bereavement as well as the intensely focused, quicksilver thoughts of people who saw everything as a means to an end. She felt the soothing gold of people who chose to simply accept and enjoy whatever their experience tossed at them, even at an airport.

It all washed over Des, leaving her gasping and clutching at her head as she tried not to crumple to her knees under the assault of these colorful emotions. Tried and failed. She felt her knees go to water as her legs gave out. Vaguely horrified at the idea of going sprawling on the ground in the middle of a busy airport, she was mostly swept away by the crashing waves—continuous, now—of what she finally accepted as other people's emotions.

But strong hands caught her by the arms before she could fall. She hadn't even sensed their owner's approach, what with an entire airport battering her psyche. He held her easily, scooping her up, duffel and all, and began carrying her toward the row of waiting seats.

"You shouldn't be traveling alone so soon after the attack."

Ah, fuck. Of course. Who else would be here to see me at

my weakest? Des rolled her eyes away from the seats to Thierry LaFours's face. He looked as brooding and handsome as ever, though she'd never seen him this desperate and irritable.

Who're you, my mother? Des was going to say. What came out instead was, "Salut, from Philippe."

And it was worth the jarring of her aching bones when LaFours, in his shock, dropped her on the seats.

"*Ow*—fuck you!" she barked, as another wave of pure hell washed over her. She closed her eyes and curled up around her duffel bag, squeezing it till she could feel the edges of her laptop, buried in the middle of her clothes. "Fuck—*fuck!*" By the time the wave passed, her face was wet with sweat and tears, and she blinked up at a worried and startled LaFours.

"How'd you know I'd be here?"

Shrugging, he knelt beside her and put the back of one hand to her forehead. She pulled away petulantly, and he frowned. "Jacob and James, of course. They asked me to make sure you got in all right. And they were right to, from the looks of you."

"You're a fucking prick."

"Does it make you feel better to believe so?"

Des huffed and closed her eyes. "Acres better. Any new leads on who took Ruby?"

LaFours sighed. "None since James called two hours ago." Another sigh. "Whoever has her got three steps ahead of us and is managing to stay there. Every time we think we've got a lead, it evaporates like water."

Des opened her eyes and blinked away wetness. "Water?"

LaFours's raised an eyebrow. "Yes. Water."

But Des was barely paying attention. She was thinking back to the capital-D *Dream*. To being pulled in a thousand different directions by a thousand different winds, attacked by a thousand different enemies, until she'd turned herself into water.

They can move you, but they can't hold you, Philippe had said. *Remember that little trick.*

Des remembered. At last, she remembered. In spite of the winds of a thousand emotional states pulling her in every direction, trying to find even more chinks in her armor, she tried to imagine herself turning into water. A *Garoul* woman, surrounded by gale-force winds tearing away pieces of her self until that self became amorphous and dancing—mutable, but ultimately of a piece.

Water.

For a moment, the winds of the feelings grew stronger and more intense. She could almost reach out with some never-used, atrophied part of her mind and touch the places from which the thoughts originated.

Water, she thought, and she tried to believe with all her being.

Water, she told herself calmly.

And water she was. The winds blew through her and tore at her, separating splashes of her, only to whirl them back together again. The winds tore through her but didn't dash her to bits as they had before. Even as she was driven into drops and jets, she always came together again, waves joining waves.

She still felt the winds of the emotions surrounding her, but they weren't as devastating or overwhelming. After a few minutes of relative calm, she peeled open one eyelid, then the other, peering out through a pained squint only to see LaFours staring down at her as if she were mad.

"I'd send you back to your brother if I thought another plane ride so soon would do you any good," he said heavily.

"You and what army?" Des croaked. She laughed, easing up on her duffel and attempting to sit. "You may be an Alpha, but you're not the boss of me. The boss of me's currently M.I.A. somewhere in Europe, assuming her kidnappers haven't moved her elsewhere." As she made her way upright, the airport attempted to spin, but Des held it ruthlessly in check. Water did not get vertigo. And it certainly did not get nauseated and puke all over Thierry LaFours's expensive neo-Victorian wear, though it would be quite amusing if water did.

"Not that this is the time or place, but what exactly is your problem with me?" LaFours asked, standing up, arms akimbo. A Yul Brynner pose if Des ever saw one.

Des huffed, despite her returning headache. *Water-water-water.* "I don't have a problem with you. I just don't like you."

"You don't *know* me."

"Don't need to." Des leaned forward on her hands and willed the world to stop attempting to spin away from her. "Don't take it personal."

"In the name of expedience, I'll endeavor not to," he said, as grim as the set of his features and completely without sarcasm. Des thought if he'd said it with at least a little sarcasm, he might be the kind of person she could get to like someday.

"What's so funny?" he asked, offering his hand as she attempted to stand. Des, of course, ignored both question and hand.

"Wanna hear about a little dream I had on my way over here?" Des paused as she regained her feet and carefully picked up her duffel. "Actually, it was more like a stroke."

Looking as if he didn't know whether to countenance what she was saying or not, LaFours nodded once. When he reached out to take her duffel, she reluctantly let him.

"So, obviously the name *Philippe* meant something to you. When I said it, you dropped me like a sack of hot rocks," Des temporized while she pulled her thoughts together—a delicate affair, since her brain, now that it had somehow managed to master the water trick, kept wanting to remember the silver light and what might be beyond it. One per day being Des's absolute ceiling on strokes, she forced herself to think of the sunnier, less stroke-causing portion of her dream.

"I had a brother named Philippe," LaFours said without inflection. He swept out a hand, indicating she should lead the way. She did, though she had no earthly idea where she was going. "We were twins."

"Fraternal?"

LaFours nodded again. "He was, it may or may not interest you to know, the last North American Loup to be placed under a *Geas* by the Council of Alphas." Still that inflectionless voice, as if he'd rehearsed his answer.

At any rate, Des had known that whatever else Philippe had *once* been, *Geas*-ridden would be one of those things. Glancing behind her, she caught a strange look on LaFours's face. But it was almost immediately gone by the time their eyes met. "Who was he bound to?"

"Me," LaFours said softly. "Tell me about this dream you had."

Feeling as alien an emotion as she'd ever felt toward Thierry LaFours—sympathy—Des let him change the subject.

And damned if she hadn't led them to the exit without deviation.

❖

Des didn't even realize she'd fallen asleep in the rental car till LaFours said her name once. She started, looking around blearily. It took a few seconds to realize where and who she was, but once she did, she focused on LaFours, who was smiling wryly.

"Any more visions?" he asked, with the air of one torn between wanting to know and not wanting to know. Des yawned and peered out the windshield. The sun was setting, and Paris looked like a surrealist dream in its orange-gold light.

"Not so much as a hint of a vision," she replied, sitting up straight and taking a longer, better look around them. "Where are we?"

LaFours smiled absently. "My hotel."

"You own a hotel? Why am I not surprised?"

LaFours snorted. "I mean we're at the hotel at which I have been staying since my arrival in Paris."

"Oh." Des cleared her throat and ignored her own blush. "Well. Thanks."

"Oh, don't thank me yet. I'm in a two-bedroom suite. You have the other bedroom, so it looks as if we'll be roomies, as they say." LaFours snorted again at the look of horror on Des's face. "What can I say? I thought you might show up here, the *Geas* being what it is. And I wanted to be able to keep an eye on you."

Des huffed. "Keep an eye on me? What am I, five?"

"No, but Ruby would never forgive me if I let something happen to you."

At this, Des's anger deflated like a punctured balloon, and she looked away from his too-earnest dark eyes. "Yeah, well. I can take care of myself."

Gritting her teeth, Des slammed the door of the car and retrieved her duffel from the backseat. LaFours emerged calmly, unhurried, like a man with all the time in the world. This only cranked Des's urgency up another notch.

"So, what leads *do* you have?" she demanded, gesturing for LaFours to lead the way.

"That's an answer best left for the privacy of our suite." Handing the waiting valet, a youngish man with flaming red hair and a sullen air about him, the keys to the rental, LaFours shoved his hands in his pockets and strode to the hotel. He did it all so gracefully, Des felt like a rodent scurrying in his wake.

❖

The hotel lobby was, of course, a nightmare of other people's weariness, impatience, and sexual excitement. Des had to scatter her watery self so much, she could barely think to save herself from being dashed on the rocks of other people's feelings while crammed in the elevator.

She sagged with sheer relief when the doors of the elevator closed behind them. LaFours gave her a worried look but led her silently to his suite, her duffel securely under his arm.

The suite was lavish compared to what Des was used to, even at Coulter Manor. But she barely took in the opulence of the suite before dragging her tired body and psyche toward the sofa in the main room. She flopped down on it and kicked off her boots and socks before swinging her feet up with a groan.

"So, now can you tell me what leads you've got?" she groaned, putting her arm over her eyes to block out the soft yellow light when LaFours switched on an area lamp.

LaFours sighed. "Nothing specific. No one specific. Factions here resent the intrusion of American-style politics into their systems of government. They resent the winds of change George represented. Hell, they still resent the changes that Callum Coulter represented, and some of those factions have been known to object rather strenuously to any changes to our most ancient traditions."

"Uh-huh. Thanks for the PoliSci introduction, Professor. But what does this have to do with Ruby's kidnapping?" Des peered out at LaFours, who'd paced over to the balcony and was staring out the glass door gloomily. "Unless you think these assholes might've kidnapped Ruby as some sort of screwy backlash to all those changes George made—"

"I don't know for certain why they might have kidnapped Ruby, nor do I have any evidence that they've done so. Unfortunately, so far all I have is my gut feeling that one of these factions is responsible. They are, in these latter days, the only ones with the sheer nerve and resolution to kidnap a Dyre, even a newly made one." LaFours glanced at Des, his face gone unreadable, his mouth a thin, unhappy line. "None of my people have successfully caught or questioned a member of these factions. No one is willing to give up any information on them, no matter how sympathetic to our cause."

Des frowned and sat up on her elbows. "These guys have people that scared, huh?"

Nodding, LaFours turned to gaze back out the window. "They're old and powerful, and indeed, something to be wary of. Their reach is long, and those who are loyal to them are utterly loyal. It's a matter of honor, that loyalty, and they would die before betraying it."

Frustrated and disheartened, Des groaned again. "Then how the fuck are we supposed to find her while she's still alive? *If* she's still alive?"

"She's still alive. She has to be." LaFours turned to look at her again. This time, his grim features had lightened just a little with hope. "And that's where I'm hoping, you'll come in handy."

Snorting, Des sat up and swung her bare feet to the pile carpet. "I'll admit, I'm pretty handy. But what the hell can I do that an entire spy network can't? When the people we're up against have vanished like smoke and even the people who are on *our* side are too shit-scared to help?"

LaFours closed the distance between them in a few short strides and knelt in front of Des, who leaned back warily.

"Once he took the *Geas*, there was no place on Earth I could go that Philippe could not find me," LaFours said fervently, his dark eyes intent and intense. "He called it his Thierry-dar." LaFours smiled a little, though it didn't reach his eyes. "I think that vision you had—"

"Or dream. It could've been just a dream. Or a stroke. A stroke-dream," Des muttered as LaFours snorted. "My dream was just a dream. A really vivid one, but a dream."

"It could have been. But I highly doubt that, as you've never met my brother, nor would you likely know anything about him. The last person to ever have taken the same oath you've taken was Philippe. That oath is witnessed and given power by the Untamed itself. And rather than see you fail at your office again, it decided to give you the help and guidance you need to fulfill it. It may have been George's time to rejoin the Untamed, but it's not Ruby's time. The Untamed wants to see her live and learn to rule. She is meant to be our Dyre.

"And you are meant to be her protector, just as Philippe was meant to be mine. And just as he was given certain abilities, so you were given abilities to aid you in protecting your Dyre until she can protect herself."

This close, Des could feel LaFours's determination and hope-edged desperation picking at her, trying to sweep her away with its fervency. Even without that...ability she'd recently picked up, she'd probably be able to feel it. LaFours wasn't doing anything to hide how anxious he was about the taking of the woman he obviously cared so much for.

Des had been feeling pretty much the same way since she woke in her own bed in the aftermath of the attack.

"Look," she began, licking her dry lips. "Say I believe the stuff your brother told me in that crazy-ass stroke-delusion-thing. Say I believe these abilities you mentioned were actually *real*, and not just me losing my ever-lovin' mind." Des finally looked away from LaFours's suddenly *very* interested gaze, though it was tough going. "How would I use something so random and fucking uncontrollable to *find* her? Seriously, *how do I find her*? I don't know that I believe the Untamed is now sticking its fingers in everyone's pie, trying to micromanage shit it never did anything about before, but I'm willing to do or believe whatever I have to—so long as there's reason—to get her back."

LaFours took her hand and squeezed it briefly, before letting go and standing up. He paced back to the balcony doors, his hands linked behind his back. "There are places in the city and just outside it where the Garoul congregate. I and my 'spy network,' as you call it, have canvassed these places and taken our questions there, all to no avail. But then, we haven't yet gone there with an admittedly untrained, but apparently powerful psychic."

It took Des a moment to realize he meant her. She bristled and shook her head. "Hey, now, I'm no psychic."

"Aren't you?"

"Well, it's not like I can see the future or read minds, or shit like that," she half lied, thinking of the faces and gabbling of strange thoughts definitely not her own that had overwhelmed her in the airport. Then she shuddered. "Maybe I'm just going schizo. It's not so beyond the pale ale here. I mean, I've already been rabid."

"You're not schizophrenic, and we both know it," LaFours dismissed, waving his hand. "Whatever it is you have, it's a leg up. Something that can help point us in the right direction, at least by letting us know who's lying and who's not." He hung his head for a moment then looked over at Des. "You said you would do anything to get her back, and I'll hold you to that. If getting her back means you accept whatever gifts the Untamed has conferred upon you, for however long it's conferred them, then I expect you to do that and use them to the best of your ability."

Des bristled for a moment then sighed, shaking her head and running her hands through her hair, pulling until the roots ached more than the remnants of her headache. "Right. Fine. You're right." She sighed again. "So. Okay, Professor X. Scouring the Loup hangouts with me using my flashy mutant powers…sounds like a plan. Better than anything *I've* got, anyway. When do we start?"

LaFours gave her a measuring glance before looking out at the city once more. "At Moon's rise. And after you've cleaned the blood out of your ear, nose, and teeth."

Chapter Two

The spray-painted sign above the blacked-out windows of the abandoned warehouse read *La Pleine Lune* in spiky silver letters. As Des and Thierry got out of the rental, their feet noiseless in the audible backbeat of the rave music coming from the warehouse, Des took a deep breath and closed the passenger side door.

Water, water, I am water...

Des had been chanting this to herself since she and Thierry stepped out of the elevator into the hotel lobby at Moon's rise. Now, as they approached the rave spot, Des could already feel the flux of hundreds of minds and psyches pushing at and trying to overwhelm hers.

She stumbled, and Thierry caught her by the arm.

"Will you be okay?"

"I'll be fandamntastic," Des said, shrugging off his hand and his concern. Even this close to the rave, no light emanated from the dusty windows. Blackout curtains, Des thought, snorting. *It's probably lit up inside like daytime.*

Just then, two clearly drunk or high people staggered out of the front doors, arms around each other for support, past a bouncer who waited just inside. A covert sniff confirmed what Des had already sensed. They were Loups.

Well, then. Maybe not like day*time…*

The two Loups staggered past Des and Thierry, the taller brunet giving Thierry an interested once-over from under shaggy fringe, the smaller blonde eyeing Des speculatively.

Des snorted again. "Fuck *off,* Frenchie."

The two Loups looked at each other and laughed. They gabbled something out in French that was too fast for Des's textbook grasp of the language. The only word she could pick out was *Americaine,* said with no small amount of amusement.

Then the pair were past, trailing laughter and booze fumes in near equal amounts, and Des and Thierry were at the door, which the bouncer, another Loup, held open for them respectfully. He even bowed to Thierry.

Des rolled her eyes as they walked in, and she was hit by a blast of music and emotions that nearly wrecked her psyche in tandem. "I take it you've been to a couple of these before."

Thierry smiled wryly, blinking a few times to adjust his eyes. "Never. But I suppose you could say my reputation precedes me in certain circles of the Loup world." Without further ado, he stepped forward into the huge, open, crowded space in which figures danced and writhed and flung themselves around. As he waded into the mass of bodies, heads turned and dancing paused, for however briefly. Whispers and admiring glances followed in his wake.

His reputation, whatever it was, had indeed preceded him.

At last, something we have in common. Des sighed and let her own eyes adjust before following Thierry into the wolf's den. Almost immediately, her senses were overloaded. She tried to call up her electronic board and dial them down, but the swirling, raw emotion that battered her and tried to sweep her away made concentration all but impossible.

I am water, I am water, I am water…

Des gritted her teeth and focused on Thierry's back as he went through the crowd. She concentrated on his intentness and singular determination as it cut through the emotional morass like a silver knife through Loup flesh.

With that small light to hold on to, she forged her way into the strobing, claustrophobic darkness.

❖

By the time Des reached the bar, Thierry was engaged in a heated discussion with a shirtless Loup with spiky green hair and matching vinyl pants. His narrow chest was covered in arcane, mystical tattoos, and his nipples and belly button were pierced. His face was also pierced at his nose, eyebrow, and lip. His dark eyes were keen and clever. And highly, highly agitated.

Perhaps whatever he's on has something to do with that, Des thought, noting the pinprick pupils and minute, random facial tics, *but the rest is probably all from dealing with Thierry LaFours.*

But whatever the reason, this Loup was arguing rather spitefully with an Alpha in the middle of a rave, as if that was something that just happened every night. Not for the first time, Des wished her rusty schoolbook French was up to parsing what was being said.

But then those pinprick dark gray eyes flicked over to her and the Loup smirked, showing too-sharp teeth. His Change was definitely near, even in this mixed crowd. And not just because of Full Moon Waning. He was high on something and genuinely angry at Thierry LaFours's gall, his absolute shamelessness in coming to him after all this time, and all that'd happened.

And on the heels of that sudden knowledge came the sharpest, most agonizing sensation of heartbreak, no dimmer or duller for being very old. Des nearly keeled over. She did, in fact, find herself leaning against Thierry as this feeling overwhelmed all the others in the immediate vicinity. It caught her up and captured her, held her close and wrapped her around in its darkness.

This is how it'll be if they kill her. This is how it'll feel all the time.

"Fuck," Des moaned as she crumpled toward the floor. Thierry caught her and hauled her straight, keeping her upright with his hands.

"And who is this?" the other Loup demanded over the music in thickly accented English, a bitter smirk on his face. "Finally found someone to replace your precious Vivienne, eh?"

Another wave of heartbreak tinged with rage crashed over her, threatened to take her over.

Thierry's mouth thinned and he glanced at Des, his face torn between worry and anger. "This is Jennifer Desiderio, the *Geas*-protector of the new North American Dyre," Thierry said lowly, lips skinned back from his teeth. "Des, this is Nicolae Korinski, Beta of the Korinski Pack, out of Poland."

"*Philippe's* Nicolae?" Des rasped out before she made the connection. She scanned Nicolae quickly, as she put aside that awful old-fresh feeling of heartbreak momentarily for surprise and wonder. Then he was scowling at Des, but with tears in his eyes.

"You…you knew Philippe?"

Des shook her head, swallowing. "I only met him briefly this afternoon. In a dream. He says *salut.*"

Nicolae actually took a step back, wonder now completely eclipsing his raw heartbreak. He glanced at Thierry, who nodded once, then looked back at Des, the tears that'd threatened to spill finally falling. He wiped them away impatiently, giving Des a quick once-over of his own.

"You're…you were the one they chose for George Carnahan as well, yes? *Le petit chiot enrage?*"

"Nicolae," Thierry said warningly, but Nicolae smiled and shook his head in disbelief and awe.

Des spoke enough French to parse out what Nicolae meant: the rabid little puppy. It wasn't the first time she'd been called that, but never non-disparagingly. In fact, Nicolae seemed…no, *was* fascinated with her. It shone out of his being like a light.

Nicolae reached out and brushed his fingers against the back of her hand. A small shock of static electricity passed between them, and his eyes widened.

"So you have it, too, do you not? The—how do you say?—talents, yes? That is what Philippe called them." Nicolae nodded, his smile trembling for a moment. "Philippe had a strong connection with the Untamed. His talents were very strong. And now he's passed them on to you."

He took Des's hands and gazed into her eyes, his own filling with tears once more, then he glanced at Thierry, that sensation of heartbroken rage making a brief comeback before settling into banked embers that Nicolae put aside with visible effort. Then he searched Des's eyes again. Finally, he smiled. "Come with me. I know someplace where we can speak privately. I'll help you in any way I can."

❖

Nicolae led Thierry and Des through the dancing crowd, nodding and hailing people as he passed. They were nearing the exit when a tall young Hume with long platinum hair, tattoos and piercings everywhere, and dressed in more ice-white latex than Des'd ever seen on one person, blocked their way.

"Nicolae—" the guy began, almost timorously. Nicolae smiled up at him and put a flirtatious hand on his arm. He leaned in close and whispered something in his ear that made the clearly anxious man blush, but relax somewhat. Then Nicolae pulled away with that satisfied smirk.

"*À plus tard. Soyez un bon garçon alors que je suis parti.*"

"*Toujours,*" Blondie said, looking at Des and Nicolae holding hands. Des was suddenly rocked back by this latex-loving stranger's jealousy and feelings of futility.

Then Nicolae was sweeping her toward the door.

In seconds, with a quick *au revoir* for the bouncer, they were out in the relatively fresh air, away from the emotional free-for-all that'd nearly swept Des under.

"So where's this place we can talk in private?" she asked warily. Nicolae squeezed her hand almost playfully, glancing back at her.

"A little after-hours bistro I happen to know. It's quiet and practically empty at this time of night. For the next few hours, anyway."

Nicolae led them around the back of the warehouse to a filled parking area, and his sleek black Lexus parked crookedly in what used to be a handicapped parking spot.

Finally letting go of Des's hand, Nicolae dug around in the pocket of his tight vinyl pants, came up with his keys, and unlocked the door with a beep. "Get in," he said, ping-ponging his gaze between Des and Thierry, who looked at each other. Thierry sighed, shaking his head and muttering to himself in French. Then he turned a rather hopeless look on Nicolae.

"Tell me, Nico, has your driving improved at all in the past eleven years?"

Nicolae's smile turned positively loupine. "Only one way to find out, yes?"

"Shotgun!" Des called, crunching through gravel to the passenger side of the car.

In less than a minute, Nicolae was gunning it out of the parking lot, nearly hitting at least three other cars on the way.

When Des heard the discreet click of Thierry's seat belt from behind her, she grimaced and quietly followed suit.

The night sped by to the soundtrack of eerie witch house music blaring from the Lexus's speakers. Nicolae drove with a lead foot and spun the wheel like he was a disc jockey several times. Before Des knew it, they were close to the center of Paris.

"Here we are!" Nicolae exclaimed, parking almost diagonally

in front of a dimly lit establishment and shutting the ignition off. Then he reached behind him for a shimmery rainbow shirt that a rather pale Thierry handed him with a sigh.

Grinning, Des let herself out of the car on legs that only wobbled a little.

❖

"So, the rumors that've been going around are true, then?"

Des and Thierry shared yet another glance. Des shrugged this time. "What rumors would those be?"

Nicolae rolled his eyes and took a sip of his cappuccino. "The rumors that your Dyre was kidnapped, taken right from your hands."

Des scowled but gritted her teeth and nodded. "It's true."

Nicolae searched her eyes and sighed. "That's rotten luck. I hope you find her before anything happens to her. I also hope I can be of some help to you, but I fear what little I know may not open doors, even if it gets you to the right ones."

Des looked around them at the sparsely inhabited, cozy space. The few people in it besides them were Humes, and they were not sitting close enough to hear what was being said. "If you can just point us in the right direction, he'll worry about opening the doors," she said as she poked a thumb at Thierry. "His reputation precedes him, or so I've been told."

Nicolae grinned and leaned back in his chair, shimmery rainbow shirt sparkling. "Indeed it does. The upstart little *Québécois* rebel with balls *and* brains, who Challenged and schemed his way to the upper echelons of power." He toasted Thierry with his mug.

Thierry ignored the toast and took a sip of his espresso, looking mildly offended. "I didn't scheme. I fought for myself and Philippe, and for others like us."

At the mention of Philippe, Nicolae's formerly merry eyes

were suddenly leavened with melancholy, and that sensation of heartbreak prodded at Des's psyche.

Water, water, water.

Nicolae looked at Des and smiled. "You really saw him?"

"Either that, or I'm going cray-cray, yeah." Des's own smile made a limp appearance. "At first, he looked like my mom, but then, I dunno, maybe I was ready to see things as they really were because he started looking like this handsome devil sitting next to me." Des nodded at Thierry, and Nicolae laughed. "He was with the Untamed, and he seemed well. Content. And he asked me to tell you both *salut.*"

Nicolae laughed again, though this time it was shaky, and his eyes had that watery, unshed-tears look. "That's Philippe, all right. Never 'I love you, Nico,' or 'I missed you, Nico.' Always *salut.* As if we were acquaintances meeting on the street." Nicolae huffed, looking down to his cappuccino. He wiped at his eyes. "If you…if you see him again, Des, please tell him that I still love him, and I still miss him?"

Des swallowed again and nodded. "Of course I will." Though she doubted that she'd ever see Philippe again, this side of the Untamed. However, with the way things were going, Des might just wind up giving him that message in person. And soon.

"Tell us what you've heard and what you know about factions here that opposed George's changes to the North American Loups' system of government," Thierry asked after a polite minute had passed. "Was there any faction that disapproved badly enough to make sure he had no direct successor?"

Nicolae snorted. "I can name you five off the top of my head."

Thierry sighed again, pinching the bridge of his nose. "Let's start with the *least* vocal, shall we? And work our way up."

Nicolae's smile grew crooked. "Well, the least vocal, though no less vehemently opposed to the so-called 'Western Upstarts,' would be the Patsonos. Though they would tie rather easily for disapproving silence with the—"

"Prevosts," Des interrupted. Both Nicolae and Thierry looked at her.

"Give the lady a prize," Nicolae said, glancing at Thierry. "And you need me for what, again?"

"Julian Prevost was staying at my father's manor, then he disappeared after Ruby, my Dyre, was kidnapped." Des pursed her lips. "He and his wife. And despite what some people might think, they're both in this neck deep."

Thierry frowned. "We don't know that Evelyn was a willing participant in this."

"The fuck she *wasn't.*" Des balled her hand into a fist, next to which her untouched hot chocolate sat cooling. "You and James Carnahan have blinders on, but you gotta take 'em off if you're gonna help me save Ruby. You can't—"

"You're truly asking me to believe that my niece in all but blood had a hand in killing her own father? And over a Dyrehood she never wanted?" Thierry demanded, his cool finally breaking, his mask of calm finally slipping. "Julian, I'll believe. Maybe even that he somehow talked Evelyn into helping him kidnap Ruby. But I *won't* believe she's responsible for George's—her *father's* death!"

Thierry's voice had been steadily rising, and now he lowered it, glancing around before his eyes came back to rest on Des. "I won't."

Des smirked. "That's cool. That's totally whatever, because you know what? I can believe it enough for the both of us."

Stubborn silence spilled out between them for so long, Nicolae began to shift. He cleared his throat and put his cool hands, heavy with rings, on top of Des and Thierry's.

"Look, let's don't argue over it till you've heard at least some of what the Families have been up to in your absence, Thierry.

And, Des, it's your job to follow your gut. Your instincts about your Dyre will be better than anyone else's." Des noted the way Thierry flinched. "But even a *Geas*-guided instinct can be wrong. You cannot always run on instinct. Sometimes, logic must be the order of the day."

"Well, logically, there's a good chance I'm right," Des muttered. Nicolae rolled his eyes.

"Ai, you're worse than Philippe when his instinct was prodding him in a certain direction. Stubborn and unwilling to see reason. Too used to following your heart, no matter how much trouble it gets you into." Nicolae let go of their hands and stood up. "Pardon me."

With that, he walked off to the back of the bistro. Toward what Des assumed was the bathroom.

For a minute, she and Thierry sat there in silence, avoiding each other's gazes.

"He's always blamed me. For Philippe taking the *Geas* and for Philippe's death." Thierry sighed again, burying his face in his hands for a few moments.

Startled and unhappy, Des bit her lip. "Is he right to?"

Thierry leaned back, running his hands through his hair. "He's not wrong. Everything I love has a habit of leaving me."

You and me, both, buddy. Des shook her head, uncertain what to do in the face of Thierry's sudden vulnerability. "I'm sure that's not true," she lied awkwardly.

Thierry laughed, a mirthless sort of bark. "The appendices of what you don't know about me could fill the Grand Canyon to overflowing, Des."

Des shrugged and held up her hands in surrender. "Whatever, dude. We don't even have time for this. The longer she's gone, the colder the trail gets. So I say we put aside who had a direct hand in George's death and work harder to prevent Ruby's. Deal?"

Thierry dragged his palms down his face and looked at Des

for long moments before nodding and holding out his hand for shaking. "Deal."

Des took his hand. And by the time Nicolae returned from the bathroom, red-eyed and leaking heartbreak like a busted faucet, Thierry was composed once more and Des had finished her hot chocolate. Everyone sat in silence for a short span, studying fingers and drinks and the table. Finally, Thierry cleared his throat.

"Tell us what you know about the Patsonos and the Prevosts," he asked quietly.

Chapter Three

Ruby stepped into the lavish but simple wood-paneled dining room, feeling very self-conscious in her rather frothy, perfectly fitting, blood-red sundress. A bunch of unfamiliar faces stood behind their chairs around the long, dark wooden table, waiting for her appearance.

She also saw the too-familiar face of Julian Prevost. He was smiling that condescending smile and radiated a mellow scent Ruby could only identify as *satisfaction.*

Still smiling, he raised a long, delicate champagne flute to her. "DyreMother."

Des is going to kill you, Ruby thought with a savage satisfaction of her own. *You're a walking dead man.*

"We mustn't linger in doorways, my dear, it's rude," Evelyn murmured from behind her, putting one gentle hand on the small of her back. Unlike her husband, the scent she radiated translated as anxiety and a very small amount of regret.

Ruby glanced over her shoulder, frowning, but all she saw was Evelyn's lovely, smiling face. Evelyn looked resplendent in her hunter green gown, like a woman who had everything to live for and be joyous about, and yet she was dead, too. They all were, once Des caught up with them. The only question was whether Ruby would still be alive to witness it. Sighing, she stepped into the dining room proper and tried to smile, to radiate nothing but calm and hope her own scent didn't give away too much.

"Julian," she said as graciously as she could. Everyone at the table, which seemed to be a mile long, nodded respectfully. For a moment she was floored, then she remembered she was, for once in her life, the highest-ranking person in the room, if not the one with the most power. She looked into each and every face present and saw some measure of respect, despite some who would not readily meet hers and eyes that met hers all too readily. Mixed in with those varying levels of respect were emotions ranging from resentment to indifference to fascination.

Taking a breath, Ruby approached the chair at the head of the table. Evelyn was quick to pull out Ruby's chair for her. With a murmured thank you, Ruby stepped between it and the table. Evelyn quickly went to her seat at Ruby's left hand across from Julian.

Aware of every eye on her, Ruby let out the deep breath she'd been unaware of holding, and sat. Cue given, everyone else around the table sat, too.

This is going to be a very long dinner, Ruby thought, already tired and her appetite gone.

❖

"So," Ruby began, initially reaching for her champagne but veering last minute for her water. The last thing she needed to be tonight was tipsy. She turned to Julian. Despite Evelyn being the one sent to tempt her, Ruby figured if anyone had the power of disclosure here, it was Julian. "Evelyn mentioned something about a way for me to pass my Dyrehood on to another Loup without me dying. Is that true?"

Julian smiled a little wider, holding up his flute as if to examine the contents. "DyreMother, we may, of course, discuss whatever topic you wish, but it is rather louche to discuss such matters as that over dinner," he replied, practically smirking.

Ruby held his gaze until his smirk slowly faded, to be replaced by a pained grimace and glance at his wife. Then Ruby smiled and examined her own water glass. "Indeed? Then please forgive me my lapse in manners. Chalk it up to characteristic Yankee bluntness, and I'll save the shop talk for after dinner when the servants have retired for the evening and the women are in the drawing room playing the spinet and giggling."

"Ah! Ha-ha-ha!" Evelyn burst out with a fake party-laugh that turned heads and made Julian wince.

Ruby trained her gaze on Julian, who stubbornly refused to meet hers. Then she looked at each and every Alpha at the table with a gaze that said, *I'm marking you. I will remember you all. I will never forget this.*

Just then, Loups in black and white servant's attire entered the room bearing appetizers that smelled of grade-A beef and some sort of tangy sauce, and Evelyn deftly steered the silence into a discussion with the Alpha next to her about the health of Julian's stable of polo ponies. Julian, for his part, continued to admire his champagne and dart veiled glances at Ruby. The rest of the table happily engaged in their own conversations, delighted to ignore the most important person in the room.

Ruby nibbled on her appetizers and regally held her peace.

❖

After a mostly tasteless five-course meal that was very meat-heavy, Julian leaned close to Ruby to murmur, "Well, if you're ready for those answers, would you care to retire to the library with me and Evvie?"

Ruby repressed a shudder at his nearness and glanced down at the rest of the table. She was still being politely ignored by everyone except Evelyn, who chatted with the Alpha to her left but kept glancing at Ruby out of the corner of her eye.

Taking another deep breath, Ruby pasted on a smile. "If I won't be taking you or Evelyn from your desserts, of course."

Julian smiled widely and he stood, bowing slightly and offering Ruby his arm. After a moment of hesitation, Ruby took it and also stood. The room suddenly fell silent. All the Alphas were gazing at Ruby once more. It was rather eerie.

They don't know how to treat me, Ruby realized, *so they're steering clear of me till this mess is resolved, one way or another. I'm a Dyre, true, but not* their *Dyre, who's notably absent. Maybe their Dyre doesn't know or doesn't approve of the efforts of these few kidnappers.*

But then the Alphas were standing as well, bowing to Ruby in the same way Julian had: deferentially, if not amusedly.

Julian cleared his throat and led her out of the dining room. Evelyn, like a bit player, silently trailed them.

❖

"What do you know of primogeniture?" Julian asked without preamble as they seated themselves in the overstuffed chairs of a library that seemed to dwarf the one at Lenape Hall. He was brooding into the depths of a snifter of sherry.

Ruby crossed her right leg over her left. "Firstborn child inherits when the parent passes away. A practice still in place within most *Garoul* societies, regarding the Death-right, with the exceptions of North America, parts of Southwestern Asia, and most of Western Africa. But for those few exceptions, it's the foundation of Loup government."

"You've done your homework, as they say."

"I've had little else to do, really."

"Hmm. Well." Julian sipped his sherry. "At any rate, you're absolutely correct about primogeniture and its place in *Garoul* society. But that doesn't mean there isn't much to be said about nurture as well as nature. Nurture also has an important place in our society, so you must already know."

Ruby blinked and looked at Julian until he looked elsewhere.

"It is for both of these reasons we've felt the need to act in a way that must seem precipitous, if not outright hostile. You see, there is a way for you to pass on your Rights and position as the North American Dyre without dying, and we need your full cooperation to make that happen."

"Yes, so I was told." Ruby gripped her armrests lightly. "And to whom would you be wanting me to pass on my position and power?"

Julian exchanged a look with Evelyn, who smiled nervously then looked back at Ruby. "To a child. One who will be raised within the bosom of the *Garoul*, trained from his earliest days to rule in the Old Way. And this child will bring about the return of the Old Ways to the New World." Evelyn paused. "And once your Rights have been passed on, you'll never have to trouble yourself about Loup affairs again."

Ignoring the part of her that wanted to leap at the chance, no matter what was involved, Ruby frowned. "And who is this child you want me to pass George's legacy on to?"

Exchanging another glance, the pair sat forward almost as one. But once more, it was Evelyn who spoke. "*Your* child, Ruby." She smiled that anxious smile again. "Your firstborn child."

❖

"Are you shitting me?" Ruby demanded after several minutes had passed with not a word from either of them. "Are you completely fucking shitting me?"

"Hear us out, Ruby," Evelyn said. "By the Right of Primogeniture, you can pass your Powers on to your firstborn child. Which is the natural way—the *Loup* way—of transferring power. It takes no more than the laying of a simple *Geas* that severs your ties to your power and transfers it to the child, who won't come into his full inheritance until he survives his Fever."

Ruby shook her head. "I can't believe I'm hearing this. You want me to bear a child to be indoctrinated into your ways, so you can make North America a fiefdom of the Old World?" She laughed disbelievingly. "I'm not even pregnant and have no plans to be!"

Julian and Evelyn exchanged another glance, and Evelyn's smile grew more nervous. "That actually wouldn't be a problem, Ruby. You see, we have a father in mind for the child."

Horrified, Ruby sat back. "Oh, my God! You people are insane!"

"Or rather," Evelyn went on as if Ruby hadn't interrupted, "he has himself in mind, actually."

Shaking her head mutely, Ruby finally found her voice after another few tense moments had passed. "Never mind who you want to breed me to like a fucking mare—why wasn't I told that primogeniture was even an option for getting out of being Dyre?"

Julian gave her a wry smile. "Likely because the Coulters either didn't realize or had forgotten. They're nothing more than an upstart branch, barely seven hundred years old. Or you were purposely mislead by the Coulters to believe there was no way out of your situation."

Remembering all the questions Des and Philomena had fielded on that same subject with honesty and no small amount of regret, Ruby knew that Julian's latter insinuation was simply not true, and she said so.

Julian shrugged elegantly. "Believe what you like, DyreMother. It isn't my job to convince you that you've been lied to, but to explain the advantages of the situation in which you find yourself."

"Kidnapped and about to be raped and impregnated?"

"Heavens, no!" Evelyn exclaimed, seemingly genuinely upset. She sat even farther forward in her chair, her eyes sincere and solemn. "You won't be forced to comply with us. Instead, you will be given a choice between the one we just explained, and...the other choice."

Ruby was repulsed by the sudden, avid light in Evelyn's eyes. "Which is?"

"The Right of Challenge will be issued. You must defend your life, your way of life, and your Dyrehood or die." Julian's smile turned ever-so-slightly cruel. Ruby shook her head, still horrified.

"But I've only been a Loup for a month! I don't know how to fight. Des had only begun to teach me, and she's my Geas-protector! She fights for me till I can fight for myself!"

Julian snorted. "That's not quite how it works here, my dear. In the Old World, the oath of the Geas-protector was only meant to act in the stead of a child, of a Loup with child, or a Loup briefly incapacitated. You will have to defend yourself here and now."

Shaking, Ruby closed her eyes for a moment and willed back tears of fear and frustration. "Defend myself against whom?"

"Against me," a soft rumble of a lightly accented voice said from directly behind Ruby. She jumped out of her chair and whirled around. He stood directly behind her chair, yet she'd neither seen, heard, nor sensed him approach. Ye gods, how had he managed such stealth? He was a compact older man in a black twill pants and a red smoking jacket. Because of that, and the combed-back gray hair and lively dark eyes, he put her in mind of a Loupine Hugh Hefner.

He stepped around the chair nonchalantly, his entire posture and air screaming man-at-leisure except for his canny eyes. They were watchful and keen. Dangerous. Ruby began to back toward Evelyn and Julian, who were, so far, mum.

She had to fight against the temptation to whine and bare her throat with all her being. She'd never experienced that before. And she knew that the stranger knew. He found her amusing.

Holding on to the flash of rage this fostered, Ruby pulled herself up out of the pit of submission and crossed her arms over her chest. She meant to look defiant, but she knew she probably only looked defensive. "And who are you?"

Smiling wider, the stranger approached her slowly, languidly, his every motion flowing, graceful, and powerful. He didn't stop until he was just outside Ruby's personal space. Then he took her hand and kissed it lingeringly.

"I am Lazslo Kiraly, Dyre of Europe, excluding Great Britain and Northern Ireland," he added sardonically, inviting her to share in the jest. "I'm also going to be the Loup who ends your reign, regardless of the choice you make within the next few days."

Yanking her hand away, Ruby took a step back. "You're here to kill me, Mr. Kiraly?"

Unperturbed, Kiraly still smiled. "Or to sire a child on you. The choice is, of course, yours."

Suddenly, completely horrified once more, Ruby glanced back at Evelyn and Julian standing with their eyes downcast and bodies in a slight bow. Their own necks were bared, though not ostentatiously.

Old World, indeed.

Turning back to Kiraly, Ruby furrowed her brow. "You're the one that wants to have a child with me?"

Kiraly nodded.

"But why? Just so that child can rule the Packs of North America and bring back your precious Old Ways, whether they're wanted or not?"

His dark, keen eyes flashed. "So that child can begin to fix what George Carnahan so carelessly ruined. So the traditions of our kind are not lost in this changing world."

At the mention of George, Kiraly skinned his lips back from his teeth and his scent became bitter, like the scent of long-buried metals. And the strength left Ruby's legs like water out of a sieve. Left her stumbling toward Evelyn's chair to sit.

"You killed George, didn't you?" Ruby asked quietly, in a high, breathless voice that sounded like someone else's. Kiraly's face, a smiling mask, didn't change by one tic. "You sent that assassin to his apartment that night to end his Line."

Evelyn gasped, and Kiraly looked away from Ruby much the way Julian had earlier. But his came back immediately, fierce and unashamed, ticking between Ruby and Evelyn.

"I should have done it many, many years ago when I saw the way his reign was trending, but I thought it would be dishonorable. A low act," Kiraly huffed. "The dishonorable thing was letting him force the New Ways onto something as old as the Moon Herself. What was dishonorable was deliberating and vacillating for over a century as his changes swept over North America and inspired other Clans to do the same.

"So, yes. It was *I* who sent the assassins. I who finally ended George Carnahan's ruinous reign." Kiraly squared his shoulders proudly. "And now, between you, his successor, and myself, as the Dyre of Europe, we can right what has been made wrong. You and I, Ruby Knudsen, can create a child that will bring back the traditions that have guided us, protected us, and kept us alive for so long."

Shaking her head, Ruby felt tears springing to her eyes once more. "No! George was all I had, and you took him from me because of goddamned politics. Snuffed out his life…his amazing life, because you're afraid of change. Afraid of innovation. Of evolution."

Now Kiraly was shaking his own head. "You don't understand, child."

"I understand perfectly." Ruby looked Kiraly dead in the eye. "Now, you understand me. I would rather fight and die for what George believed in—for what *I* believe in—than bear your child and see it turned into some puppet ruler who drags the Garoul back into the Stone Age."

The surprise on Kiraly's face and in his smug, certain scent was almost as filling as a good meal to Ruby. She was frightened out of her mind but adamant. She would rather die upholding George's dream than live because she'd let herself out as an incubator for this petty little dictator's spawn.

And perhaps Kiraly could smell this determination in her scent, because his smug mask slipped away. But then it was back almost instantaneously, as if it had never gone. The low, mean reek of him still nearly bowled her over.

"You are shocked by recent events, so I'll put your poor choice down to that and give you a few days to come to your senses and see this really is the best way for all of the Garoul," he said softly.

Ruby served his own languid, annoying smile back to him. "Come back in a few days, and I'll be even more certain. My choice is made. Whenever, wherever. I'll fight."

Kiraly's smile turned frosty. "No, you'll die. And well before the battle is truly engaged. For your own sake, please take the next few days to think over your choice. Julian. Evelyn."

And Kiraly strolled out of the library as silently and stealthily as he'd come.

❖

After that lovely exchange, no one had anything left to say. Evelyn offered to escort Ruby back to her room, but even during that walk, both Evelyn and Julian seemed to be preoccupied with their thoughts.

They passed no one, not even a servant as they made their way through halls and rooms. The hewn, well-lit halls were empty, and it couldn't have been more than nine o'clock. At

Ruby's door, Julian bowed absently, and Evelyn kissed both of Ruby's cheeks, her eyes wide and pained as if she didn't know what to say. As if she'd completely lost the plot of her day. Of her life.

"Give it some thought, eh?" she asked softly, squeezing Ruby's hands. "Within the year, you could be living wherever you want, doing whatever you want, with more money than you could ever spend. You could have the life you've always wanted." Evelyn shook her head. "I know we haven't known each other for long, but you're rather endearing, and I wish to see you be well and happy."

Suddenly, Ruby found herself thinking of Des and Thierry, Jake and James, Winkin' and Blinkin', Nathan, and poor Philomena, and tears came to her eyes.

"That's just it, Evelyn. If I said yes to Kiraly, I'd never be happy. I'd never get the life I want. And I'd always know and have to live with the fact that I betrayed the people who've done nothing but protect and teach me. And care for me." Ruby searched Evelyn's lovely eyes and saw a sense of shocked betrayal, yes, but also determination. The same stubbornness that had been George's hallmark. But then, George hadn't been so stubbornly loyal to someone like Kiraly, Ruby was certain of that. No shared ideology could have convinced him to put himself in the hands of someone who'd killed a member of his family.

Perhaps Evelyn's always been this way…or perhaps life *has made her so lacking in notions of real honor and loyalty. Perhaps she's become this way because of time and exposure to people who hold real honor and loyalty cheap,* Ruby thought with a pang. Because, above all else, this was George's daughter. Ruby wanted nothing more than to believe she could be saved? Redeemed? Turned around?

But as she looked into those lovely, devastated-but-trying-to-hold-it-together eyes, Ruby saw nothing she could save, redeem, or turn around. Evelyn obviously did not regret or doubt her choices even after hearing Kiraly killed her father. Even if she could forgive that, how could she possibly look past it?

Ruby smiled, and the smile felt sad but real. She leaned in and kissed Evelyn's cheek. "Thank you, so much," she murmured. Evelyn touched her hand to her cheek, clearly surprised. "For what? Kidnapping you? Holding you here against your will?" she asked wryly, putting her hands on her slender hips. "For forcing you to contemplate a life-or-death decision?"

"For being so kind to me while doing so. For worrying about me, and for caring about whether I live or die."

Evelyn looked startled once again, as if she didn't quite know what to say. Ruby's smile firmed up, and she stepped into her cell and closed the door. A few moments later, the lock on the outside engaged, and Ruby sighed.

❖

After trying for what felt like hours to sleep, Ruby went out onto the balcony and watched Moon-Waning travel across the sky. She thought about her father, and for the first time in a very long time, allowed herself to think briefly about her mother. But while thinking of the former brought her comfort, thinking of the latter made her as confused and angry as usual. So she pushed away those thoughts. Glancing at the moonlit ocean below her, she wondered what her father would do, were he in her position.

"Where there is life, there is hope" had always been his motto. And Kiraly's way certainly offered that, if nothing else. A life, of sorts, divorced of everyone she'd come to care for. What kind of life would that be? To be an outcast? To be utterly alone in the world?

Ruby had been alone in the world after her father had died and until she met George, but she had no choice in those matters. If she took Kiraly's offer, the responsibility would be hers. She'd have no one to blame, no one to hate but herself.

But I'm not ready to die! A very large, very vocal part of her quailed. *I haven't even really lived! I've never gone anywhere except wherever I am now, and I've never done anything except be kidnapped and used as a pawn!*

Ruby leaned on the balcony railing and sighed wearily. She was more scared of having to fight to a bloody, violent end than she was of death itself. Bleeding out the last of her life, crossing over into whatever afterlife awaited Loups on the wings of agony. To have that agony be the last fruits her life yielded would be singularly awful. Unbearable.

And yet those were her two choices. A lonely life without honor and her family—yes, she thought of them that way, even after so short a time spent among them—or no life at all.

But what about Des? Or Thierry? Surely they'll come for me.

Snorting, Ruby sighed again. "Assuming they could find me in time. Assuming they could batter or connive their way into this citadel."

Still gazing into the water, she thought about a third option of the long drop and sudden stop of self-annihilation. Ruby doubted even a Loup could survive that fall. It looked to be hundreds of feet down. From that height, hitting the water would be like hitting cement.

Tears rolling down her face, she finally turned away from the Moon's light and went back into her posh prison cell. As she lay down and closed her tear-filled eyes, she reached deep inside her for something she couldn't define. Something as wild at heart as a forest, and as bright as the moon. She reached, all unknowingly, for the Untamed Heart, and bent all her being on one, desperate wish: *Des, Thierry, please. There isn't much time left. Come find me before it's too late.*

❖

"…best bet might be trying to get in to see Kiraly in person," Nicolae finally said with a tired shrug. It was almost four in the morning, and the bistro—which, it turned out, he owned—was closed and empty but for the three of them. "If anyone can aid you in finding your Dyre, it's another Dyre."

Thierry sighed. "I was unable to procure an audience with your Dyre, Nico. His beta was most evasive as to when I might be able to get such an audience."

"Mm," Nicolae murmured. "Bertrand was always such a pompous little shit. He's probably just exerting the relatively small amount of power he has in an attempt to inflate that already massive ego." He snorted. "Kiraly probably doesn't even know that you need to speak with him."

Des pounded her fist on the table and both men jumped. "There has to be some way to get to him. Where does he live? Where are his offices, if he has them? What places does he like to go?"

Nicolae sounded amused. "Do you mean to stalk my Dyre? Track him, like a wolf tracks a deer?"

Des set her jaw. "If that's what it takes, yes."

Nicolae laughed. "In that case, I shall do my best to assist you. As far as I know, Kiraly is a recluse. He has his own private island he rarely leaves. Where, exactly, that island is, I don't know. I've never even seen the man in person." Shrugging, Nicolae leaned back in his chair and scratched his chest. "Bertrand, of course, would know, but he would never tell you. However, I know some Alphas in France that have been steadfast friends of the Dyre's since before he was the Dyre. They might be useful."

"And if this secret island's been so closely kept, who's to say they'll tell us?" Des demanded.

Nicolae grinned. "Oh, they won't. But they may be willing to get the Dyre's ear for us. If Kiraly can at least be contacted, that might help your cause exponentially. He is, to put it crudely, the grease your wheels need to get to your Dyre."

Thierry and Des glanced at each other. Then he sat forward, his eyes intent and his face a mask of determination. "And you can get us an audience with these Alphas?"

"I can try. The Korinski Pack isn't the most powerful on the continent, but it is one of the oldest and one of the best liked, if I may say." Nicolae preened. "And I'm a beta, whatever else I am. If I stop by on business, the Alphas will likely be willing to listen, if not help us."

Des and Thierry shared another glance. Des shrugged and Thierry nodded. "It's a start. It's a definite start," he said. "Thank you, Nicolae."

Nicolae waved his hand dismissively. "It is my nature to be of help to an Alpha. A leopard cannot change his spots. And anyway, it's what Philippe would have wanted. I'm certain of it."

Thierry opened his mouth to reply to that, his Adam's apple bobbing with repressed emotion, but Des never got to hear what he said because in that moment, she had another vision.

And though she didn't realize it at the time, it came on the back of her second *petit mal* in twenty-four hours.

❖

Des blinked and found herself in a different place. A place like a dream.

This room understated and elegant, yet hinted rather loudly at the opulence of the entire house: the furniture was all light-colored wood, with buff marble accents, a balcony that was larger than Des's bedroom overlooked what could only be some ocean. Des saw a large sectioned-off study complete with a big writing desk and a small library that was nearly empty. In the main room was a vanity with a mirror almost as big as the writing desk, an armoire that seemed taller and broader than James Carnahan, and a bed that could've slept three strangers comfortably.

But there seemed to be only one person in that bed, hugging the edge closest to the balcony, tossing amidst the expensive-looking cotton sheets and huge pillows.

"Ruby?" Des breathed, stepping toward the bed from her place next to the vanity. She was quite certain that when she got close enough to touch, Ruby would vanish like some sort of fever-dream.

But Des approached the bed, and if anything, this dream-reality seemed to solidify, becoming as real as her next breath. The woman in the bed, clad in a sheer, strappy white nightgown, came into sharp focus as if she was somehow more real than the room around her.

When Des got to Ruby's bedside, she found herself kneeling and reaching out gently to brush Ruby's messy curls away from her furrowed brow and face.

The moment she did, Ruby opened her eyes wide, immediately fixing on Des.

"Heyya, gorgeous," Des said around a sudden frog in her throat.

Ruby took a breath, and a tear rolled down the side of her face. "Are you real?" she asked in a tiny, hopeful voice. "Am I dreaming?"

Des smiled and brushed her fingers down Ruby's cheek. "I think the answer to both those questions is yes. But don't ask me how."

Ruby frowned and sat up slowly, looking around. Then she buried her face in her hands and began to weep. "I'm still here," she sobbed quietly. "Even in my dreams I can't escape this place."

Des stood up and sat on the bed next to Ruby, pulling the weeping woman into her arms. She felt warm and soft and real. She accepted Des's arms around her with a silent gratitude that made Des feel a thousand feet tall, even as she felt like dirt for letting Ruby get taken.

"I'm so sorry, baby," Des found herself saying in a voice

that quavered and broke as she buried her face in Ruby's hair and rocked her. "I fucked up again. I'm so sorry."

Ruby sniffed and sat back to look at Des with red, swollen eyes. "It's not your fault. It was Evelyn and Julian. I still can't believe it. And they were right under our noses—"

"My nose. And I let them take you." Des shook her head, ashamed. "Moon Above." She shuddered and ran her hands down Ruby's arms. Ruby shivered and blushed, suffering Des's pat-down to make sure bones were whole and no lacerations had, though it was tough to tell in the slippery nightgown Ruby wore. "Are they mistreating you?"

Ruby shook her head no.

"Good. At least as good as can be expected. Fuck!" Des wiped at her eyes impatiently. "Goddamnit!"

Ruby laughed a little. "If you kept a swear jar for all the times you swear, you'd be one rich werewolf." She reached out and brushed her chilly fingers across Des's cheek.

Des mustered up a smile from somewhere and kissed her fingers. "I'd have a fleet of Ferraris by now, betchyer ass."

Ruby laughed again, and in that moment, she was the loveliest woman Des had ever laid eyes on, beautiful and brave, sweet and sincere. She made Des feel pangs in places that even Holly never had, pangs that had nothing to do with fucking and everything to do with the way her heart beat faster whenever Ruby came into a room, and the way she found herself always wishing she could do more for and give more to this woman she'd barely known for a full Moon.

I love you more than I've ever loved anyone, *Des would have said had she been able. But when she opened her mouth, what came out was, "Are you frightened?"*

"Not really," Ruby lied, cupping Des's face in her hand for a few moments before withdrawing reluctantly. Then she sighed. "They haven't so much as touched me. Yet." She caught Des's

cold, nervous hands in her own. *"They're gonna Challenge me. Soon. There's nothing I can do about it, except fight. And I won't win."*

Des searched Ruby's eyes and found certainty, resignation, and great sadness. Horror washed over her like a dash of ice water. She wanted to open her mouth with a denial. A reassurance. A promise of rescue. But she didn't. *"Right of Challenge?"* she asked. *"With a newly turned Loup?"*

Ruby nodded once. *"They really want someone they can control running the North American Garoul. And that Loup isn't me. And it won't be my child, either,"* she added quietly.

Des shook her head again, looking at Ruby's abdomen. *"Child? What—?"*

"But listen, I want you to know that I love you. You've become my sister, my teacher, and my best friend. The best I've ever had. I only wish I could've been a better friend to you. Could've had a chance to—" Ruby broke off, looking away, out the balcony door, her mouth firming into a grim line. *"This wasn't your fault. It was Evelyn's and Julian's, and that bastard Ki—"*

Des blinked on the word bastard, *and everything went dark.*

❖

A moment later, she opened eyelids that suddenly weighed thousands of pounds and seemed to be superglued shut. Her mouth tasted like old pennies and she was lying on something so hard it could only be the floor.

Finally, she got her eyes open. Thierry stared down at her with worried, dark eyes, and Nicolae dabbed at her nose with something wet and cold. Des weakly swatted his hand and the wet-cold-something away, and tried to sit up. But Thierry put his hands on her shoulders and stopped her. "You had a seizure of some sort," he said calmly, belying the look in his eyes. "One moment we were talking, the next you were on the floor, twitching like a frog on a hot skillet. You've been out for nearly half an hour." Then his face took on a hopeful look. "Did you have another vision?"

Des groaned and tried to sit up again. This time, Thierry frowned but let her. "Both barrels. Ruby," she added, seeing Nicolae's face fall a little at no mention of Philippe.

Thierry brightened. "Is she—was she all right? Could you see anything that might tell us where she was?" His usually calm voice had hints of strain around the edges.

Des shook her head no once and the room began to spin. "No. Just that it was on some island. She didn't know where," Des croaked out, one hand going to her head.

Thierry put one hand on her arm, his face a study in desperate hope as she looked at him. "You spoke with her?" he asked.

"Yes," Des admitted hesitantly. "But you won't like what she had to say. A Right of Challenge will be issued to her. I don't know how long till that happens, but it's not gonna be long. I think she's got a day, maybe two. Guys, we've gotta step up our game before that Challenge is issued."

"Moon Above," Thierry breathed, pinching the bridge of his nose, seeming devastated.

"*Merde*," Nicolae whispered, sitting back on his heels, looking unpleasantly floored.

"Fuckin' A," Des agreed, snatching what turned out to be a wet dish towel from Nicolae and dabbing at the annoying trickle of blood in her ear.

Chapter Four

Several hours later, after the sun had come up, Des found herself riding shotgun in a car once more. This time, Thierry was driving. In the back Nicolae mumbled to himself and ran tarot spreads with a hand-painted deck the likes of which Des had never seen before. All the faces that peopled it had the long, canny faces of Loups, and some of them were in full Loup form.

"This is very strange," Nicolae kept murmuring in his French-Polish accent. Then he'd run another spread. "I don't understand this. It's not making any sense."

"No surprise there." Des snorted. She put about as much faith in the occult as she did in politicians.

"The cards keep taking me in circles." Nicolae suddenly gathered them all together off the backseat, shuffled them with his long, deft fingers, and put them back in a pouch, which he stuffed into the breast pocket of his leather coat. He looked like a different man with the green washed out of his meticulously parted and gelled-back black hair, and retainers in all his facial piercings. He had covered his tattoos, and he was wearing a tailored blue suit under his brown leather coat.

"I don't know what to tell you," Nicolae said. "My Alpha will likely help you in any way she can. It will be—how do you say—no skin off her nose to get us in to see at least a couple of the Alphas who knew Kiraly before he was Dyre. But as for what will happen during those audiences, I cannot tell you. And I cannot tell you whether or not we'll find your Dyre in time," he said miserably. "Sorry."

"Thank you for trying," Thierry said in all seriousness, and Des snorted again, watching the traffic behind them in the side mirror. It was bumper to bumper, just like traffic in front of them. Des had to fight to keep herself from being swept up in the frustrated anger and weariness of the drivers around them, and mostly managed.

In the hours since her vision, Des had cleaned up, changed clothes, and eaten breakfast that tasted like sawdust to her distracted senses. Thierry and Nicolae had talked about which Alphas would seem the most receptive and which Alphas would likely toss them out on their asses, assuming they even made it past the front doors. Des had contributed nothing to the conversation. She stared off into space, trying to conjure up whatever state of mind would bring her another vision.

She knew next to nothing about meditation but tried to meditate anyway. Tried to clear her mind and see Ruby as if she was right in front of her. Imagined the sweet smell of her hair and the curve of her smile, the softness of her skin and the gentleness of her manner.

Sighing, Des closed her tired eyes. The next time she opened them was when Nicolae slammed the back passenger-side door shut. Ahead of her loomed a neat brick town house, which Nicolae approached without hesitation, using a keycard to let himself in. He held the door for them patiently.

Ignoring the headache that'd been with her since Charles de Gaulle, she sat up and glanced over at Thierry, who was watching her with grave consideration.

"I think it would be wisest to let Nicolae do the talking for this particular meeting. I think you'll find he catches more flies with a little honey than you might with American bluntness," he said tactfully, and Des smiled a little.

"You are such a fucking prick, you know that?" She gave him the finger, and he rolled his eyes.

"Case in point."

Des rolled her own eyes and opened her door, levering her tired body up and out of the car.

❖

As it turned out, Des didn't get to say anything at all to the Korinski Alpha. She didn't even get to see her for most of their time there.

She was left to cool her heels in the reception area, where a pretty secretary chatted on the phone in Polish while she did something or other on her computer. She radiated complete satisfaction and relaxation that soothed Des's nerves. Bored, Des tuned up her hearing, trying to find out what was going on in the Alpha's office. Absolutely no dice.

Must be soundproofed, she thought, reaching for the magazines on the tasteful glass coffee table. They were all written in French and all about business, except for one back issue of *Vogue*.

Settling in with the *Vogue*, Des closed her eyes again, and was, this time, aware as she began to drift off.

❖

Des was in a shower.

That in itself was alarming after being in an office just a moment ago, but even more alarming, the body she was rinsing on autopilot was not her own. It was too curvy, generous of hip and breast, and too tall. Too dark.

Curious but unafraid, Des finished rinsing off soap and looked around the shower. To her right was a glass door with a gold handle. She reached out slowly, surprised yet not surprised when the arm that was hers for the moment obeyed.

She turned the handle and the door opened silently, letting out steam and moisture. Stepping over a small riser, Des padded barefoot into the bathroom proper, heedless of the water dripping and running off her in rivulets. Across from the shower was a fogged mirror, and Des reached out and planted her hand smack in the center before dragging it across the surface.

In the small, clear swath she'd made, Des could make out dark eyes and café au lait skin, water-drenched curls, and a full, curving mouth quite unlike her own spare one.

Ruby? Des thought, again both shocked yet not. I'm Ruby?

Just then, Des heard a distant but firm knocking sound. Startled, she turned her face away from the mirror toward the door leading, she presumed, back into the bedroom.

Then Des faced the mirror once more, Ruby's eyes wide and uncertain, her nostrils flaring. She caught a scent she didn't recognize, male, and powerful like the Forest from which they all had come.

Frustration and dread reaching a sudden apex, Des reached out to the mirror once more. She began to write with her index finger in the steam on the glass, a quick, brief message she hoped would last long enough for Ruby to see. And when she was done, Des let Ruby's arm fall and stood back, so to speak, in their shared body.

She began to back away from the mirror, one hand coming up to her mouth. The knock on the door sounded again, and Des yelped when her back touched the cooled glass of the shower. She took a step forward again—

❖

"—time to go, sleepyhead," a familiar voice said.

Des was jolted out of sleep by what, she knew not, only that her head was pounding and she felt as if she was about to vomit.

She struggled up out of a serious slouch as her stomach turned over threateningly. But in the seconds it took to get upright, the nausea passed. She looked around with bleary, red-tinged vision, wondering why the left side of her face felt slightly numb. Then she tried to stretch, and realized it wasn't just the left side of her face, it was the entire left side of her body.

"Oh, Moon Herself, you're bleeding again," Nicolae said worriedly, whipping out a clean handkerchief. Thierry, standing beside him, did the same. Behind them stood a tall, hatchet-faced woman in expensive business wear. She was staring at Des like she was a two-headed puppy.

Nicolae pressed his handkerchief to Des's upper lip. Des quickly took it from him and dabbed at her ear. She could already feel blood trickling down her neck.

Des looked around at the people surrounding her and licked her dry lips before aiming a fake smile at the hatchet-faced woman.

"Migraines," she said dismissively, shooting Thierry and Nicolae a hard look, before she faced the Loup she presumed was the Korinski Alpha. "Had 'em all my life."

"They must be awful," the Alpha said with rather professional sympathy. Her voice was softer than her face, light and low. She was staring at Des as if she was a sideshow. "If you like, I do keep acetaminophen in the office, if that would help."

"It wouldn't, but thanks anyway," Des said hastily, easing herself out of the chair to her feet. Her head began to throb, and the taste of blood in her mouth brought that nausea back.

Des took the arm Thierry offered as the room started to spin persistently, nauseatingly. They made their way out of the reception area, to the front stairs, and down to the car. Thierry was helping her into the passenger side when Des noticed Nicolae was not with them.

"Where's Nicolae?"

"His Alpha wished to speak with him alone," he said as he shut the door. By the time he'd gotten in and started the car, Des's fuzzy mind came up with another question.

"He isn't coming with us, is he?"

"Not any longer. His Alpha's condition for helping us was that the Korinskis be left out of it from this point on. And that includes involving Nico." Thierry's mouth was a grim, hard line.

"Fuck, that's...*fuck*," Des sighed, feeling rather down. She'd somehow gotten used to Nicolae's upbeat quirkiness. She considered him a strange, but trustable ally. To have him suddenly taken away was upsetting.

But considering what she and Thierry were getting themselves into, she honestly couldn't blame his Alpha. Though she desperately wanted to know what Nicolae would have made of this latest vision, and that Des had been *in* Ruby's body, controlling it.

Nicolae, he of the occult leanings, tarot cards, and instant belief that Des was having visions instead of hallucinations brought on by psychosis, would certainly have had an interesting take on it all. Des would have given almost anything to hear it. She was *sad* that he wasn't going to be with them anymore, and she had a feeling that Nicolae was as unhappy about this parting of their ways, as well.

Des looked up at the third-floor windows visible from their parking space. As Thierry pulled out, a pale, suited figure came to one of the windows and raised one hand in farewell. Des did the same. She supposed the chances were good she'd never see Nicolae again. If she'd known it was going to go down like *this*, she'd have said a better good-bye than appropriating the man's hankie.

❖

Ruby, shaken and suddenly chilled, stood alone with her back against the shower door reading the words on the mirror over and over, until they were no longer visible.

we'll find you. hold on.—des

Then the knock on the door sounded for maybe the third or fourth time. Ruby crept up to the counter and, after a moment of hesitation, wiped away the last of the message that'd appeared between what had felt like one blink and the next. It couldn't have, though. She was out of the shower and drying. What happened in that blank space? Crazy or not, it wouldn't do to have whoever was at her door see that missive.

Screwing her courage to the sticking place, she donned her bathrobe and hurried into the main room just as the lock disengaged and Lazslo Kiraly let himself in, smiling.

❖

"We have to get her out of there. Now."

Thierry closed the door to their hotel room and looked wearily at Des.

"I know that, Des. But other than begging for scraps and clues from the few Alphas who *might* be willing to help us, how do you suggest we go about doing that?" He sounded as tired as he looked. He sat on a sofa with a heavy sigh. Des paced for a few moments then kicked Thierry's feet out of the way and sat on the coffee table in front of him.

"It was different, this time. The vision." She paused, trying to find the right words. "I was where Ruby was, but it was different. It was like I was in her head—no, in her body. I could control it. Do stuff with it. I wrote her a message on her bathroom mirror.

Told her we'd find her if she just held on for a little while longer. Don't make a liar of me, Thierry. Please."

Sighing again, Thierry sat forward, covering his face with his hands. "These visions are fascinating. From a theoretical standpoint, the implications are tremendous. But so far, they have been less than helpful in pinpointing where she is or who might have her, Des. I fear the only thing that will get us to her is old-fashioned detective work."

"Damnit, we don't have time for that!" Des jumped up and began pacing again. "Someone was knocking on her door when you guys woke me up. Maybe the person responsible for all of this."

Thierry frowned. "And you think this person was coming to hurt her?"

"He didn't smell like puppies and good intentions."

Thierry leaned back for a moment, covering his eyes. Then he took his hand away and pinned Des with an intent, piercing gaze. "Do you think that you could do it again? Be where she was? Maybe help her protect herself from him?"

Des stopped pacing. "I dunno," she admitted, and it tasted like ashes in her mouth.

"Are you willing to try?"

Des took a deep breath and nodded again. "Just call me Psychic Stroke Girl."

❖

Once alone in her room of the suite, Des kicked off her shoes and flopped on the bed.

She immediately closed her eyes and tried to get to that place between sleeping and wakefulness. She thought it wouldn't be terribly hard as tired as she was, but instead of drifting off, she was wide awake and too worried to even half sleep.

"God-fucking-damnit," she finally breathed, sitting up. She was irritated, but she had an idea. "Thierry!"

He immediately let himself into her room, his eyes worried but hopeful. "Did it work? Did you go?"

"No. I'm too wired to do it. Too worried." Des shook her head and smiled wryly. "But I thought of a way you could help me. One you might actually like."

Thierry looked utterly confused. "I'll help in any way I can. Tell me what you need me to do."

Des, swung her legs over the side of the bed and stood up, planting herself squarely in Thierry's personal space. "I need you to hit me, not quite as hard as you can."

❖

For the second time in as many hours, Des found herself in a body that wasn't her own.

This time she wasn't in the shower, and she wasn't alone. She was scrambling backward on the huge bed she recalled from the night before, obviously trying to avoid the advances of an older Loup with a determined, but otherwise pleasantly bland look on his long, tanned face.

"You'll be saving your own life, not to mention the souls of everyone in your Packs," he said matter-of-factly as he kneeled on the foot of the bed. "If you won't make the sensible choice, Perhaps I should make it for you."

Des hit the headboard of the bed, and looked down at Ruby's—body. She was wearing nothing but a wildly askew bathrobe. She had no obvious weapons on her person, of course, but since when did Des need weapons to fight the good fight? She had tooth and claw, cunning, and blood-lust.

Des skinned Ruby's lips back from her teeth and looked up at the still-advancing Loup, who'd paused in his journey up the bed as if sensing a change in the air. His nostrils flared, and his eyes narrowed. Des froze for a moment, wondering if he'd be able to smell her or somehow sense her in Ruby's body. He was old and obviously powerful. It might not be beyond the pale.

But when he couldn't put a finger on what had changed, he shook his head and started moving forward again, smiling his bland smile once more. "I would advise you not to fight me. In the end, I will have my way, whether you're alive to see it, or not," he added, in a strange accent that sounded vaguely like Nicolae's.

"You're awful sure of yourself, ain'tcha?" Des rolled to the side and to Ruby's feet as he sprang forward in a leap that would've pinned Ruby to the bed.

Standing on the firm mattress, Des crouched into a ready-stance, face scrunched in a snarl. "Rapist motherfucker. You like picking on newly turned girls, huh? Well, let's see if you brought your A-game, toda—shit!" Dodging a leap that seemed to violate the laws of physics, Des found herself hitting the floor hard, the wind knocked out of her. She didn't bother with trying to get it back or with sitting up. Instead she scrambled out of the way and narrowly missed being pounced on again.

Fuck, this guy is *fast.* Like a spider, *she barely had time to think as she rolled to her feet.* My only advantage so far is that he's trying to capture, while I'm fighting for what feels like my life. Fuck!

Des scrambled away from another impossible leap, the fucker grinning as if he was having the time of his life. She wondered if she dared attempt Changing with Ruby's body.

But then, he'd simply Change, too, and he might very well be the faster of the two of them, leaving Des at more of a disadvantage.

Growling her frustration, Des crouched in another ready-stance as she faced him and he faced her, grinning, grinning, grinning. He was—ugh!—hard enough that the crotch of his pants was distended.

No way he's putting that thing in me, or in Ruby, *Des thought grimly, preparing to leap. No fucking way.*

Des feinted left then right as fast as she could before driving up the middle straight for him. He easily blocked her roundhouse kick with a stunner of a judo chop to Ruby's calf that left Des limping to the side warily, growling in the face of his only slightly winded smile.

"You are delightful," he murmured, laughing, getting into a ready-stance of his own, hands curled into loose fists. Des forced herself to ignore the pain in Ruby's slightly numb leg and put just enough weight on it so she could rush him. She counted on Ruby's extra height and extra weight to make tackling him worth the probable injury. One had to be willing to risk injury or even death to win a fight.

Who dared, won, *as Nathan was fond of saying, and Des had always dared much.*

But this time, her efforts didn't pay off. Before she could block it, he hit her with a right cross and everything went dark, then light again, and Thierry's concerned face hung over her own.

"What happened? Did you go? Did you find out anything else that might—"

"Shut up and punch me again!"

Without another word, he did. Everything went dark once more, in a sky full of stars and a great flash of pain. My fucking nose! Why'd it have to be my fucking nose? she thought.

Then once more there was light, but it was suddenly blocked out by a body hoving into view over her. Before Des could get away or attempt to punch out the menacing figure, it'd gotten between Ruby's legs and pinned Ruby's wrists tight to the floor, dragging them both up above her head where he held them with one hand. His other hand disappeared.

Des growled as she located the hand once more, sliding up her thigh, as she crawled with revulsion. He laughed with a patronizing, startlingly heartless tone. "Really, do stop being melodramatic, Ms. Knudsen. It's for everyone's good, and you know I'll not hurt you…much."

"NO!" Des roared, kicking Ruby's legs up and out to no avail. In fact, it only seemed to let him get closer. When Des looked down Ruby's body, she could see his hand go to his crotch. "Fuck you, motherfucker! Get the fuck off me!"

"In due course," he said lightly, fondling himself and leaning down to bite Ruby's exposed left breast. His teeth were sharp, and Des gasped as trickles of blood ran down the curve of Ruby's breast. He turned his attention to her nipple as she closed her eyes and yanked futilely in his grasp.

This is happening, *she thought in something too numb and disbelieving to be horror.* This is actually happening to me. Better to me than to Ruby.

And in that moment, she prayed for the first time since she was very little. She prayed to the Moon Herself for the strength to bear it, and that nothing knocked her out of Ruby's consciousness before it was over. She prayed—

Suddenly the teeth closing on Ruby's nipple were gone.

Daring to open her eyes, Des saw his angry look of surprised disbelief. He leaned down, pressing his face to Ruby's throat as he inhaled deeply.

"No," he said firmly then said it again, after sniffing once more. He sat up and looked at who he thought was Ruby, looked down the length of Ruby's body then back up. His eyes narrowed meanly.

He slapped Ruby's body in the face and pulled her up, not terribly hard and certainly not hard enough to knock Des back to her own body. He dragged Des to Ruby's feet, shoving her at the bed hard.

The wind once more knocked out of her, Des tried to roll away. But he was on her again, his weight on her legs, delivering another stinging slap before pushing Ruby's legs apart.

Des started to sit up, and this time, he punched Ruby in the chest hard enough that Des coughed and saw stars. While she fought to catch her breath around the intense pain, she could see, his head between Ruby's legs, cocked to the right as he sniffed her.

Des weakly struck out with Ruby's leg, kicking at his head. He swatted her leg absently and kept sniffing. By the time Des was able to struggle up to Ruby's elbows, he'd withdrawn and stood up, his arms crossed angrily. He glared at her as if she'd done something wrong and offensive.

Faster than Des could process, he had leapt on the bed and yanked Des forward by Ruby's curly hair.

"Do not even imagine that this is over, Ms. Knudsen," he breathed, hot and heavy on her face before shoving her back down to the bed.

Head ringing from slaps and yanks and lack of adequate oxygen, Des lay there for a few moments when the door to the room slammed open and shut, the lock engaging with a final click.

She turned her head toward the door to make certain Ruby's attacker was truly gone before struggling onto her side, then upright. Ruby's legs wobbled but carried Des across the room to the big writing desk.

The desk was heavier than it looked—heavy enough to give Loup-strength a run for its money, but she managed to move it across the room. By the time Des got it to the door, she didn't give two shits. She settled it in front of the door with a solid thud, then leaned against it, breathing hard and sweating.

Looking down at the desk, she spotted something that hadn't gotten jostled off in all the pushing and jouncing of the desk: a fancy ink pen in a holder that appeared to be bolted to the desk. Rifling through the drawers, Des came up with a pad of plain paper. After thinking for a few moments, she quickly jotted down a message and left the pen and pad where she'd dropped them.

She staggered into the bathroom, shedding the hopeless bathrobe and avoiding the mirror on her way to the shower.

Under the hot spray, Ruby's left breast stung. Everything stung, especially Ruby's face. Gentle prodding of it revealed a black eye and split lip that'd be healed probably within minutes.

Des sighed and leaned against the marble wall of the shower, tired and relieved and terrified. Ruby's wobbly legs finally took her to the shower floor in a slow, sliding slump, and she curled up in the corner under the hot, everlasting spray. She closed her eyes, but the tears leaked out anyway, only to become part of the spray running down Ruby's face.

Somehow, some way, after a while, during which the pain in Ruby's face lessened, and finally went away completely, Des drifted off...

❖

...only to gasp into wakefulness, bolting upright, one hand flung out defensively. Then she was swinging at someone who appeared at her side, his own hand held out as if to touch her.

"Don't!" she croaked, scrambling away from the hand and clumsily off the other side of the bed. Her left side was more numb than it had been last time, her speech slightly slurred. Even the vision in her left eye was blurrier.

But she could swear it was him again, until she blinked away the last of her disorientation, and it wasn't. It was Thierry LaFours. And she wasn't in that ornate, awful bedroom, but in her bedroom of the suite she and Thierry shared.

"I'd ask if you were all right, but you're clearly not," Thierry said hesitantly. "How was Ruby? Could you talk to her? Was she in immediate danger?"

"Betchyer fucking ass she was in immediate danger!" Des scrubbed her face with clammy, shaking hands. One hand came away bloody. "Fuck, I'm bleeding again."

Thierry tossed her a wet washcloth.

"Thanks." She wiped at her face and her ear. "When I got there, some asshole was trying to force himself on her. I think he was an Alpha."

Thierry's mouth dropped open in shock. "An Alpha? What makes you think that?"

"He was way stronger and way faster than anyone I've ever personally faced except for maybe Nathan." Des shook her head and sat on the edge of the bed. "He beat me. Without even breaking a sweat. He could've had us, but he stopped for some reason. Kept sniffing Ruby's body, and getting angrier and angrier. Then he stormed out." Dropping the washcloth on the bed, Des sighed again. "I barricaded the door with the writing desk and left Ruby a note telling her what happened. It was the best I could do."

Swatting angrily at the tears running from her eyes, Des didn't even notice Thierry coming to sit next to her on the bed until it dipped slightly under his weight.

"You did good," he said gently. "The best that could be expected, under these increasingly strange circumstances."

Des sniffed and hung her head.

"But tell me, would you know this Alpha again if you saw him?"

"Fuck, yeah."

"Good, that's good. Would you possibly be able to pick him out of a bunch of photographs?"

Des looked up at Thierry, puzzled. "Yeah, I guess. Why? Do you have photos of every Alpha in Europe?"

Thierry smiled his grim smile.

❖

Ruby blinked and Kiraly was gone. In fact, all she saw was the hot, stinging drops of water pelting her face.

Spluttering out water, Ruby blocked the spray with her hand and stood up carefully, her body vaguely tired and achy. Once her face was out of the spray, she looked around to see the same shower she'd used over the past couple of days.

Impossible, except...

"Des," she murmured, shaky-voiced and hopeful. She quickly turned the shower off and stepped out, looking for a message on the steamy mirror, but she didn't see one. Disappointed and worried, Ruby turned to the open door and suddenly remembered Kiraly. Nearly stumbling over the torn, disarrayed puddle of her bathrobe, Ruby picked it up and held it in front of her body as she peered out the door.

No one in the bedroom, though the bed was a mess. Ruby remembered Kiraly had propositioned her again. This time, he hadn't seemed willing to take no for an answer. He'd trapped her near the bed and advanced on her.

Ruby sniffed, dropped her robe, and wiped at her wet face, too apprehensive to leave the bathroom. Then she noticed the writing desk wasn't in the study where it was supposed to be. It was in front of the door to the bedroom.

"What the—" She rushed out of the bathroom and grabbed the lamp from her bedside table. She brandished it toward the study, thinking she was barred in with her would-be rapist... only there was no one in the study. Just a trail of office supplies through the bedroom to the door.

And who could have done it—who *would* have done it, but Des? She'd fought off Kiraly or talked him out of doing what Ruby had suspected he'd come there expressly to do, and barred the door just to make sure he couldn't get in again.

Almost smiling, Ruby looked around the messy room, and that smile began to fade.

Only, what if Kiraly had done what he'd come there to do, and Des hadn't been able to stop him? He was, after all, an Alpha of Alphas, a Dyre. What if he'd...overpowered Ruby's body while Des was in it, and Des, being who she was, had suffered being raped so that Ruby wouldn't have to?

Oh, granted, Ruby didn't ache anywhere she'd associated with sex, her limited experience aside, forced or otherwise. But with Loup healing time, that might not mean anything. And who knew how long she'd been blinked away.

Ruby shuddered and was on her feet and en route to the bathroom before she consciously realized feeling the need for another shower. The fact she'd come back to herself already in the shower was very telling, indeed. She passed the door to the room and the desk, and she happened to glance down at an unfamiliar pad of paper with writing on it.

Shuffling closer, Ruby picked up the pad and mouthed the words as she read them, tears filling her eyes.

he tried to rape us. i fought as hard as I could and he got the drop on us anyway. but then he stopped. i don't know why. don't move the desk or he'll try again. who is he? alpha?—des

Ruby was relieved for herself, but she was heart-sore for Des, who must've fought hard, then been bested and nearly... Ruby shied away from the awful, awful thought. She wiped her eyes and, under Des's big, blocky print, wrote three words in her own looping cursive:

Lazslo Kiraly. Dyre.

❖

Thierry retrieved his laptop from his bedroom and brought it back to Des, who was lying down once more.

Now that she'd had a moment to notice, her head was killing her, to the point of nausea. All she wanted was to sleep, but...

Not until Ruby is safe.

Thierry sat on the bed next to Des and placed the laptop in her lap. He had a face cued up, but it was unfamiliar. Des looked for the NEXT field and clicked it. Same shit, different day.

She sighed, rubbing her tired, aching eyes and forcing back nausea. "How many Alphas are there in Europe?" she asked Thierry, who snorted.

"Two hundred and twelve, as of two days ago. And, of course, the Dyre makes two thirteen," he added. Des groaned.

"My eyes'll up and explode well before I get to number *one* thirteen!"

"Nevertheless, this is the fastest way to find out which Alpha you saw. And as you say, time is at a premium."

"Yeah. Right." Des remembered the reason her entire body felt like shit. And she remembered that she'd endure a hell of a lot more for that reason. She'd endure *anything*...

She clicked the NEXT field. Another unfamiliar face.

"Who's to say the Alpha who has her is from Europe?" Des asked suddenly, and Thierry looked pained.

"I have an extensive database with dossiers on every Alpha in the world."

"I'd ask how many that is, but I don't think I want to know."

"You probably don't. Keep looking, and I'll send down for room service."

"I want a bacon cheeseburger, rare, onions, pickle, and fries. Oh, and mayonnaise on the side," Des added. Despite the nausea, she was starving. "And a strawberry milkshake!"

"I'll be sure to relay that to the kitchen, madam," Thierry said sardonically.

Des smirked briefly...and kept looking at pictures.

❖

"Ruby, darling, it's Evelyn."

Ruby started, then sighed, rolling onto her side facing away from the door. "Go away, Evelyn!"

"I would, but I'm worried for you." Evelyn paused, then

went on in a lower voice. "Dyre Kiraly mentioned that he'd been round to see you and, well, are you all right?"

Sniffing and thinking of Des fighting off Kiraly and losing, thinking of the way her body still ached from a fight she hadn't been present to take part in, she closed her eyes on the spectacular view the open balcony doors afforded her. Tears burned the backs of her eyelids and threatened to trickle out from under them. "I'm fine!" she called.

"Forgive me, darling, but you don't sound or smell fine. I can smell your distress from here. Won't you let me in, and we'll talk?"

Ruby snorted, opening her eyes only to roll them, then swiping impatiently at the tears. "What's there to talk about, other than how everyone's favorite Dyre tried to rape me but settled for roughing me up instead?"

Silence. For nearly a minute. "Ruby, dear, Dyre Kiraly may have been a bit aggressive in his attempt to woo you over to our cause, but—"

Before she could stop herself, Ruby sat up and swung her legs over the side of the bed, then marched toward the desk-blocked door. "Don't you dare, Evelyn. Don't you dare make excuses for what he's done! If that's all you're here to do, then we really do have nothing to say to each other!"

"But, Ruby—"

Ruby leaned against the desk, suddenly exhausted—physically, mentally, and emotionally. "Your boss came in here and tried to rape me, Evelyn. If De—if I hadn't fought him off till he came to his senses, who knows how far it would have gone?"

Evelyn's sigh was gusty and tired as well. "Dyre Kiraly means well, he really does. It's just that sometimes he can be..."

"A raping asshole?"

"Ruby, please."

Ruby snorted again. The idea that the person on the outside

of a locked jail cell would feel the need to plead with a prisoner was laughably ironic.

"Listen, Ruby. Dyre Kiraly told me about the baby, and I simply wanted to check on you and extend our sincere apologies for any distress we may have inadvertently caused you. But if you'd simply told us from the start—"

"Baby?" Ruby demanded, frowning and turning to face the locked door. "What baby?"

Another silence for another minute. "Ruby, darling, you're pregnant. Didn't you know?"

Ruby's mouth dropped open, and her hands instantly went to her abdomen, stopping just shy of touching it. She shook her head and let her hands drop to the desk. "You're insane," she said angrily. "In case he didn't tell you about how his attempted rape ended, it was just an attempt. Kiraly didn't impregnate me, nor will he ever."

There was yet another long silence, one that Evelyn broke only when it sounded as if she was speaking from right against the door. "Ruby, the child is not Dyre Kiraly's. It's someone else's." Evelyn paused, then went on delicately. "The night before your first Change, you had an assignation with Uncle Theo, did you not?"

That's none of your business! Ruby meant to say, but the implication of Evelyn's words hit her the moment before she spoke, and her righteous indignation deflated like an old balloon.

"You...you think I'm pregnant with Thierry's child?" she asked quietly, almost meekly, her hands hovering near her abdomen once more.

"We don't think, Ruby. We know," Evelyn said heavily, with another sigh. "It's in your scent now. Dyre Kiraly smelled it when he came to see you. Your scent is already changing, even though it's only days into the pregnancy. To the noses that would smell it, your scent proclaims that you're a mated female with child."

"But this is impossible. Thierry and I were only together one night. I can't be pregnant! And we certainly didn't mate. Not the way you mean! We haven't even been on a date!"

"You're not thinking like one of the Garoul, Ruby," Evelyn said patiently. "It's only recently that even the upstart North American Loups began to have assignations for recreational purposes only. But still, like the wolves we came from, The Garoul typically mate for life. Uncle Theo has been paying court to you, has he not?"

"No! I mean, yes! I think...but—we're not—" *Mates. And I'm not pregnant. I can't be.*

"Ruby, dear," Evelyn lowered her voice even further, and Ruby leaned over the desk, closer to the door. "Whatever your future arrangements with Uncle Theo, right now you must accept you are pregnant with his child. And," Evelyn took a breath, "that the child you now carry may very well be our salvation. Yours, mine, the entirety of the Garoul society."

"What?" Ruby blurted out, then closed her eyes on the beginnings of what was promising to be a spectacular headache. "Assuming I am pregnant, what in the hell are you talking about, Evelyn?"

"Simply this. If you're willing to pass your Right to Rule onto your firstborn, the child you now carry, and let Dyre Kiraly have the raising of the child, he would be willing to let you go free after the birth of the child, and you'd be able to live out the rest of your life in comfort and happiness with Uncle Theo, if you so choose."

The puzzle pieces were falling neatly into place, and Ruby was once more horrified. This time, when she rested her hands on her abdomen, they stayed there protectively, possessively. "You want me to give up Thierry's baby—my baby—to be raised by that, that monster?"

"Ruby, you're not thinking clearly. This is the opportunity

of a lifetime for the child to be raised with all the advantages of being the heir of two Dyres and raised in the full traditions of the Garoul—"

"I'd rather see my child raised by someone who loved him and who didn't threaten to murder his mother than raised in this gilded cage with that conscience-less lunatic you call Dyre," Ruby spat.

This time, Evelyn was silent for so long, Ruby thought the other woman had left. She was just turning away from the desk and door, however, when Evelyn spoke again, anxious and desperate. "This is for the best, Ruby. Surely you must see that?"

"Must I?" Ruby wiped at her eyes. "And how happy will this comfortable life you think I have ahead of me with Thierry be when he finds out I sacrificed his child to save my own skin?"

"I honestly think he'll be so happy to have you back and alive, he'll forgive whatever means secured your return to him," Evelyn said softly. "Uncle Theo's never been lucky in love. He's lost so many people that have been dear to him over the years. I don't know that he could take another large loss in his life."

"And the loss of a child isn't a large loss?"

"Not as large as the loss of the woman he loves."

"He's only known me for a month!"

"But do you doubt that he loves you with all that he is?"

Ruby hung her head, tears forming in her eyes. She didn't answer. She couldn't, because she feared that answer. Feared what it meant for her future, for if, as Evelyn had said, she and Thierry had mated for life, what did that mean for her and Des?

I care about Thierry, I do. But I'm not ready to settle down with him. I might never be, Ruby thought with sudden understanding, though it was like a dagger in her heart. *I don't think that I'm in love with him. Not the way I am with Des. She infuriates me and confounds me, drives me to distraction and drives me insane. And there's no one I trust more, no one I miss more. No one I love more. She would do anything for me and I would do anything for her. Absolutely anything.*

But on the heels of that thought, Ruby's hands tightened over her abdomen. If there *was* a child… Ruby felt a wave of fierce protectiveness and determination wash over her. If she had a child, she would always put him first. Even if that meant giving up Des.

But what if it means giving up the child to Kiraly? she thought with sudden horror. *What if I keep resisting him, and he kills me after the baby is born and then kills the baby? All because I didn't cooperate with him now? I don't know how, in good conscience, I could cooperate. But how can I, in good conscience, risk my child's life? At least if he's raised by Kiraly, he'll be alive. He'll be safe and taken care of. He'll always have everything he wants or needs.*

"Except a mother who loves him," Ruby murmured aloud, crying again as that feeling of a dagger in her heart increased one thousand fold. It doubled her over for a few breathless moments and left her gasping.

"What was that?" Evelyn asked as Ruby drew a deep breath and straightened up slowly. Her whole body was shaking minutely.

"Nothing, I just…" Clearing her throat, Ruby turned away from the door and leaned back against the desk, still breathing as deeply and slowly as she could. "How can I trust that if I give my baby to you willingly, you won't kill me and more people I love?"

Evelyn's voice, when she spoke, was wry. "I could give you my word and Dyre Kiraly's, but I don't suppose those are worth much to you."

"You suppose correctly."

"Then I'm afraid you have no guarantees we'll stand by our word," Evelyn said with that same wryness. "But we will. I'll see to it personally. And a year from now, when you're living the life you've always dreamed, you'll see that we were right about everything."

Ruby closed her eyes again and thought about the life of which she dreamed. It'd changed so much from the life she'd dreamed of having even two years ago, and certainly more than the life she dreamed of ten years ago, when she'd been dealing with her father's death and Casey Hampton had entered her life.

The life Ruby now dreamed of involved days spent with her new friends and family, Jake and Jamie, Winkin' and Blinkin', Des and Thierry, and this new person who was apparently growing inside Ruby.

But that life would never be. There were sacrifices to be made, and Ruby was the only one who could make them, despite Evelyn's chumminess and concern.

Wiping her eyes with one hand, the other rubbing soothingly across her abdomen, Ruby took a shaking breath and let it out slowly.

"Evelyn?"

"Yes, dear?"

"I need time to think."

A much briefer silence, followed by Evelyn's voice, brimming with restrained hope. "Of course you do, darling, of course. I'll leave you to it, shall I?"

"Thank you."

"You're quite welcome."

When she was certain Evelyn and her super-sniffer were gone, Ruby sagged down to the floor, her back against the desk, and wept.

❖

"How's it coming?"

Des looked up from the screen and took the last sip of her

milkshake. Thierry stood framed in the doorway, clearly reluctant to disturb her. But Des waved him in, moving the remains of lunch to her other side so he could sit.

"It's going. Badly. I've gone through this thing twice. No dice."

Thierry sighed. "Well, the only thing for it is to widen the search parameters. Our Alpha is not European. Perhaps the United Kingdom?" He looked at Des questioningly, and she nodded.

"I mean, he looked European. Very Old World. But I guess searching the U.K. couldn't hurt. I mean, the guy damn sure wasn't from Africa or Asia."

Thierry turned the computer to himself and typed something that made the laptop beep. Then he turned it back to Des with a new face on the screen.

"You'll be pleased to know the U.K. only has forty-seven Alphas," he said. Des snorted.

"I'll be pleased if one of them turns out to be the asshole we're looking for, anyway," she corrected him. "Moon Herself, help us if he's not an Alpha. But I don't see how he could've beaten me so easily, otherwise. And even an Alpha shouldn't have been able to take me down so easy—" Des's eyes widened, and she sat up.

"What is it? Have you thought of something?" Thierry asked, bringing that singular focus to bear on Des.

"Maybe. I mean, he might have beaten me so easy because he was old and had years of fighting and power behind him, yadda-yadda, yeah, totally possible, super-likely. Or maybe he beat me so easy because he's more than an Alpha. Maybe he's an Alpha of Alphas."

Thierry paled. "Maybe he's…" He hesitated, as if afraid to say out loud what they were both thinking. Maybe their kidnapping problem was bigger than advertised.

"Let me pull up the dossiers on the Dyres," he said, taking the laptop from Des, who crossed her legs in *zazen* and sat forward, wide-awake and with a strong feeling that they were, finally, on the right track.

A few seconds of clicking and typing, and Thierry turned the laptop back to her. The first Dyre was clearly not the one she was looking for, being the Dyre of West Africa and about twenty shades too dark.

The next face to pop up was Ruby's. The photo was candid, but obviously taken while she was unaware. But she looked so unbearably fragile and lovely.

Des quickly clicked to the next one. South American Dyre. And while Esteban Santiago had the right complexion, the friendly, round features and black hair knocked him out of the running for the asshole who had Ruby.

Next.

Des's mouth dropped open because she hadn't quite believed that a Dyre, of all people, would attempt to harm another Dyre, no matter how opposed to that Dyre's reign they were. The Right of Challenge and Contest that followed it was one thing, but kidnapping and attempted rape?

"That's him." Des turned the laptop to Thierry. "That's the Hugh Hefner-looking motherfucker."

Frowning, Thierry sighed. "That's the European Dyre, Lazslo Kiraly."

"The guy with the secret island somewhere no one knows?" Des pinched the bridge of her nose like Thierry tended to. It didn't help. "What're the odds he's got Ruby there, right now? Fuck!"

"I can't believe Dyre Kiraly would do something like this." Thierry said, sounding lost and unconfident for once. Des smacked his arm to get his full attention.

"Well, believe it, pal, because that's the guy I saw. Believe me, a person doesn't forget the face of the guy that tried to rape them." She shook her head. "The question isn't whether or not he did it. Because he did. He took her. The question is how do we get her back from him?"

Thierry ran a hand through his hair and blinked repeatedly. "I...I don't know. It never occurred to me that we'd be up against a Dyre, let alone *this* Dyre."

Just then they heard a knock on the door. Frowning, Thierry excused himself and went to answer it, muttering about someone named Remy possibly having more intel. Des, meanwhile, shrugged and turned the computer back to herself, studying the face on the screen. The bland smile and iron-gray hair. The dark, somehow empty eyes.

Suddenly Des leapt to her feet, dumping the laptop on the floor. She heard the sharp chuff of a bullet leaving a silenced gun, then the muffled thud of a body hitting the carpet in the main room. Footsteps quickly entered the suite.

Des hurtled toward the door, meaning to slam it shut, but she was too slow. Before she got to the door, a figure appeared in the doorway, backlit by the brighter light of the main room. Then she heard another sharp chuff was slightly different than the last. As something sharp pricked her neck, Des knew why.

Fucking tranq-gun...not again...

Once more, as they had four days ago, her limbs went from sluggish, to heavy, to completely numb, only much, much faster. She was unconscious before she even hit the carpet.

PART II: THE CHAMPION AND THE CHALLENGER

Love couldn't be moved by circumstance, poor choices, or even blatant lies—skewed and damaged, yes, but the heart couldn't deny what it wanted most once the desire was planted. Whether in bliss or affliction, love owned you all the same.
—Rachael Wade

CHAPTER FIVE

"Welcome back to the land of the living," a familiar voice said. Des, in the midst of groaning and stretching, sat up instantly, her eyes wide open and immediately falling on the sight she'd only seen in visions for the past week.

Ruby.

Tired-looking, worried, a bit gaunt, but *Ruby*.

Despite pervasive lethargy, Des opened her arms, and Ruby immediately went into them, laughing and sobbing just a bit. She was warm and soft, shivering in Des's arms.

"Moon Above, is this for real? Am I really here?" Des asked, glancing down at herself and around the bedroom before closing her eyes and simply enjoying the embrace she'd been wanting for what seemed like forever. She closed her eyes and inhaled Ruby's exotic shampoo and sweet, slightly musky scent, which was vaguely different than Des remembered. Now it was very faintly salty, like the ocean smelled from a distance.

Probably from being cooped up here, for so long, Des thought, letting go to look at her...and cup her beloved face in her hands. Ruby smiled, bright and big.

"You're really here, Des, though I wish the circumstances were different," she said, that smile deflating just a little. "They brought you here this morning. I could smell it was you, and I knew they weren't lying when they said they had you here. I moved the desk, and they brought you in. Dumped you on the bed like a sack of potatoes." Ruby shrugged, her gaze drifting down to Des's collarbone. "You were out so deep, I thought you were dead at first."

"Never, without a fight," Des promised, hugging Ruby again, tight and close. Ruby allowed it for a few seconds before pulling away. This time, she wouldn't meet Des's eyes. "What? What's wrong? I mean, besides the obvious?"

Ruby brushed her curls behind her right ear and took a deep breath. "That's kinda why they brought you here, Des. To fight for me against Lazslo Kiraly, the European Dyre. To be my champion."

Des nodded grimly. "That's the way it should be," she said, yet she practically quailed inside, remembering how easily he'd beat her last time they'd met. "I'll fight him for you and win."

Ruby smiled, a little watery, a little sad. "I know you would, Des, but that's not the only option."

"What other option could there possibly be? They wanna end George's Line. That means ending you," Des said, shrugging. "Simple as that."

"Actually, it isn't that simple. They only want to destroy George's legacy as the option of last resort. Their plan A, so to speak, is for me to pass on my Right of Rule to someone they can control," Ruby added, still not meeting Des's eyes. Des reached out and tilted Ruby's face up till their gazes finally met.

"Sweetheart, that means killing you."

"Or..." Ruby turned her face away again. "Or I could pass my Right along the old-fashioned, traditional way."

Des's brow furrowed. "I thought that was the old-fashioned, traditional way."

Ruby smiled again, but it wasn't so big or bright, this time. "That's the second-oldest way. The oldest is through primogeniture."

"Cream of *what*?"

Ruby laughed briefly. "No, primogeniture. It means that all power and rights are passed on through birth. To the firstborn child."

Des quirked an eyebrow. "Buuuuuut you don't have any children."

"Not yet, no." Ruby took another deep breath. "But they want me to. They want a puppet they can put on a throne to rule the way they want him to rule."

And in that moment, a few pieces connected for Des. Namely, the real reason why a Dyre would try to rape another Dyre, never mind one as lovely as Ruby.

"That was why Kiraly was trying to do what he did." Des shook her head. "He wanted to get you pregnant. Wanted his heir to be on that throne."

"Yes."

Des's face scrunched up. "Ew. Just...ew. That slimy fuck." She searched Ruby's upset, exhausted face, then reached out and caressed her cheek gently. "But he didn't do it. He stopped before he could. Wait, why'd he stop? I mean, yay he stopped, thank the Moon Herself, but why? An attack of conscience?" Des snorted cynically. "Yeah, sure. I'll believe that in about a thousand years. No, there had to be some other reason. A guy like that doesn't just stop out of nowhere."

"No, he doesn't."

Des nodded. "And as glad as I am that we're both un-raped, I don't like not knowing why. It sure as shit wasn't my ninja-like skills," she admitted bitterly then tried to put a smile on the face of it. "But when it comes time to win the Challenge, babe, don't worry. I will. I haven't lost one yet."

"It might not even come to that, Des."

"What? Of course it'll come to that! It definitely ain't goin' the other way! Kiraly's coming near you over my dead body!"

"Actually he wouldn't have to come near me, Des."

Des snorted. "He'd have to unless his aim was really spectacular."

"Des!" Ruby's eyes filled with tears and she looked away again, but didn't dislodge Des's hand. "You don't make it easy to tell you—" She broke off, her eyes overflowing, her voice breaking.

Des leaned in and kissed her cheek, the tip of her nose, and finally, her lips.

The kiss was only meant to be a comfort, but it became something else in short order. Ruby's breath huffed gently into Des's mouth, followed by a timid tease of tongue. Des moaned and took control of the kiss, clenching Ruby's biceps and pulling her closer. Ruby slid her arms around her waist, and her body practically melted against Des's.

"You're making it so hard to tell you…" Ruby gasped out as Des maneuvered them both down to the bed.

"Tell me what? Moon Above, but you feel so fucking good." Des kissed into the skin of Ruby's throat as she settled on top of her and wrapped her long legs around her waist. She slid her hand up one of those lovely legs, under a ridiculous, frothy red sundress, even as her kisses wended their way back up to Ruby's mouth. "Oh, fuck, yeah."

"God, Des, we can't. Not here, not now."

Des sat up a little to look Ruby in the eyes, even as she brushed her fingers across Ruby's labia and Ruby gasped again, shivering all over. "If not now, when?"

Ruby looked up into Des's eyes, searching them before making a tiny little sobbing noise and turning her face away again. Des took this as her cue to stop and did, with surprisingly little frustration on her part. Ruby, however, looked very frustrated and extremely regretful. "I'm sorry, Des. I want to, but—"

"It's okay, you don't have to explain. You wanna stop, we'll stop." Des said gently, surprised at her own patience. Ruby laughed mirthlessly.

"That's just it, I don't want to stop, but I can't, in good conscience, keep going." She sat up, pushing Des off her.

Des flopped down to the bed, putting one arm over her eyes, tamping down the sudden, intense jealousy as something occurred to her that threatened to swamp her relative calm. "Is it because of Thierry LaFours?"

Ruby sighed softly. "Partly. See, just before they brought you in, Evelyn told me why Kiraly stopped when he did. Why he didn't rape me—you—us. It's because I'm already pregnant."

Des froze as the bottom dropped out of her stomach. "How? I mean, I know how—when? Who—oh, shit," she sighed, knowing even as she asked.

Ruby's voice took on a broken, slightly muffled quality. "Unless it was an immaculate conception, it happened last week. I slept with Thierry and only Thierry. He's the father. And I guess Kiraly could smell that I was already pregnant, somehow. Or is that even possible? Does being pregnant really make a woman smell different? And so soon? Was Evelyn telling the truth?"

Des nodded, remembering that she'd noticed that faint, ocean-salty scent under Ruby's normal one. Tidal and primal and faint, but there. "I could smell it on you when I woke up just now, only I didn't realize what I was smelling. Just that I'd smelled that scent before on Phil, only a billion times stronger. Of course, with everything that's going on, I didn't put two and two together."

"Oh, God. Oh, Des, I'm so sorry. I didn't know that. It was just one night, and I didn't even think to—"

"It's not your fault." *It's Thierry LaFours's fault for not using protection.*

"I should've thought ahead then. If I had, I suppose I'd be pregnant one way or another, and it'd be Kiraly's child instead.

But even though it's not, they say if I pass along my Right to Rule and give them the baby, they'll let you and me go." Ruby's voice broke again despite an unhidden attempt to keep it firm, and in seconds, she was sobbing. "If I don't, they'll make you fight, and he'll kill you, Des! Then they keep me here, take the baby when it's born, and kill me, too. But at least if I give him what he wants, it'll save our lives."

Des finally removed her arm from her face and looked over at Ruby. She saw the woman she loved weeping into her hands like a brokenhearted child, far too young to be carrying a child herself. For a moment, Des saw only someone she'd lost forever, someone that Thierry LaFours had won by dint of knocking up. But that moment passed, and she saw, first and foremost, the woman she was bound to protect. To sacrifice for. Even die for, if called.

And Des knew she would, no matter whom Ruby chose to share her life with, no matter whose child she carried. She would fight for Ruby's life and the life of Ruby's child. For Ruby's right to share a life with Thierry LaFours, if Ruby so chose.

Her own heart breaking, but quietly, invisibly, Des sat up and wrapped her hesitant arms around Ruby's shaking shoulders. Ruby stiffened for a second, then went limp, turning to hug Des, her face buried in the crook of Des's neck.

"Don't worry, sweetheart, I swear, it'll be okay. You'll see. I'll fucking ice that old bastard, and you and the baby'll be safe. I'll fix everything." *Or I'll die trying...*

"But how?"

"I dunno, I'll figure something out," Des promised, squeezing Ruby tight. "I won't let anyone harm you or your baby."

"But I don't want anyone harming you, either!" Ruby started sobbing again on Des's shoulder. Des laid them both down again, pulling Ruby into her arms, letting her cry herself out. "I don't want anyone to be hurt! And not because of me!"

"Oh, people are gonna get hurt, unfortunately. But it won't be because of you. It'll be because of their stupid politics and greed. I'm gonna kill 'em, Ruby. I'll kill 'em all, then we're going home."

❖

They lay in bed like that, and Ruby cried herself to sleep. Ever the guardian, Des kept watch over her, holding her close until she heard a clicking noise from the direction of the half-moved desk and the door to the room.

Des carefully eased out from under Ruby and got out of bed. She was surprisingly steady for someone who'd been sedated till an hour ago. When the door opened, she had already put herself between Ruby and whatever menace waited on the other side. The "menace" turned out to be a tall, slim blonde, who could, with that wavy hair and those canny blue eyes, only be George's daughter.

"You must be Evelyn Prevost," Des said politely. The woman nodded, turning on a smile that might have charmed most but did nothing for Des.

"And you must be Des."

"Someone's gotta be."

That movie-star smile turned almost genuine and Evelyn's scent, muffled by a light perfume, was amused. "Ellie said you were a card," she murmured, letting herself in all the way and closing the door. She was wearing a soft green sundress similar in cut to Ruby's.

"Funny, because he also said that *you* were an innocent pawn in all this shit. Now, why do I think that's not so true?" Des crossed her arms and watched Evelyn stalk across the room on long, supermodel legs past Des and toward the balcony. But instead of going outside, she sat on the chaise just beyond the open doors and patted the space next to her for Des to sit. Des snorted.

"Thanks, but I've spent enough time off my feet in the past few days."

"Ah, of course." Evelyn crossed her legs, her demeanor gone from almost flirty to businesslike in the space of seconds. "So. I won't waste your time charming you. I'll simply get right to it, shall I?"

"I think that'd be best."

"All right, then. I need you to talk Ruby into giving the child she carries her Right to Rule, and then giving us the child." Evelyn's smile disappeared. "Not only will that save your life, but it'll save hers."

"So she told me."

"Ah. And?"

"And what? You can take your compromise and shove it up your ass. I'm not letting you take her Right to Rule and her child just to save my own skin. And as for Ruby, who's to say you won't kill her as soon as you have what you want from her?"

Evelyn sat forward intently. "You have my word, and the word of the Dyre of Europe."

Des snorted. "The word of a kidnapping patricide and a would-be rapist and child stealer? Gee, well, let me get right on that whole 'trusting you' thing."

Flinching, Evelyn sat back till she was leaning against the wall, her face turning slightly red. "I did not kill my father. I merely—"

"Save it for someone who cares, *chica*. 'Cause I can assure you, that ain't me." Des sniffed the air, then rolled her shoulders, ready to throw down if the bitch wanted to. It'd be a warm-up for the main show.

Evelyn narrowed her eyes and she sniffed the air, too. She finally held up her hands in placation. "I'm not here to fight."

"I am. Or didn't you get the memo from the child-stealing rapist?"

Flinching again, Evelyn sighed. "Listen, I care about Ruby. Rather more than I expected to."

"If you cared about her, you wouldn't have brought her to this place. You wouldn't be threatening her life and the safety of her child."

"Dyre Kiraly doesn't do things the way I might, it's true, but he really only has the best in mind for the North American Packs."

"And he'll steamroll anyone who gets in his way, isn't that right?" Des clenched her fists, wanting to deck Evelyn Prevost but unwilling to make any move that'd possibly put Ruby in more danger. "Fuck him and fuck you."

Evelyn smiled coldly and stood up, pacing around Des in a wide circle. "Does it feel good to keep throwing what's really quite a generous offer in my face?"

"Generous?"

"I was the one who talked Dyre Kiraly out of simply having her dispatched and then sitting back to watch civil war consume the Packs of North America. I was the one who talked him into accepting under his tutelage the child she now carries. I saved lives, and all you can do is castigate me for things that weren't my fault! Whose life have you saved lately?"

"I dunno what 'castigate' means, but I sure as fuck blame you for choosing the side of the people that killed George. Your father," Des huffed, tracking Evelyn with her senses, ready for anything. "I blame you for what's happening now, and I'm damn sure gonna make you pay for it, if it's the last thing I do. And I don't care whose daughter or sister you are."

Evelyn's pacing faltered, then stopped. "Ellie still believes me. Believes in me," she said defensively from behind Des, who turned to face her.

"Yeah, well, Ellie loves you. I don't."

Evelyn turned away, one hand on her hip, the other at her temple. "This is going nowhere."

"I agree. Perhaps you should leave."

"Perhaps I should." Evelyn's shoulders slumped only a little before coming back up. "Bear in mind, however, that your next visitor will be Dyre Kiraly. And when he comes, he'll issue a Challenge to Ruby. Unless you talk her out of it, she'll accept. And since she's pregnant, you'll have to fight in her stead. You will, of course, lose."

"That seems to be the consensus," Des said, shrugging without apparent interest.

"When you lose, Ruby will be kept here till the child is born. She will be killed after that. Whether or not Dyre Kiraly will stand by his decision to raise the child as his own is anyone's guess. He can be...mercurial."

"As Dear Leaders tend to be."

"I don't want to see that happen, Des."

"Then help us get outta here!" Des demanded in a whisper, letting some of her desperation show. "Or tell someone where we are. Please. Before this Contest happens. Kiraly needs to be brought to account for what he's done, for what he's doing. You *all* do, and somewhere inside, you know that, Evelyn!"

Evelyn shook her head and stalked back toward the door. "We're doing what's best for the Packs. For the world. You and Ruby are collateral damage. Unfortunate but unavoidable. At least if you can't talk her into cooperating." At the door, Evelyn looked over her shoulder at Des. "*Please.* Talk her into cooperating. She can still live out a full, happy life. With you. Wouldn't that be lovely?"

Yes, it would. "Not at the cost of our world and everything we hold dear. I'd never sell out my Pack or the Packs just for my own personal happily ever after. Neither would my Dyre."

"You're both willing to die for an ideology?"

Des tilted her head disbelievingly. "You're willing to kill for one. Does that make any more sense?"

Evelyn flinched again, but didn't reply. A moment later, she was gone, nothing to show she'd ever been there but the click of the lock.

Des stared at the door for a while before going up to it and moving the large desk back in front of it. Then she got back into bed with Ruby, who didn't so much as stir. She must have needed the rest badly. Des couldn't blame her. She pulled the heavily sleeping woman back into her arms. And in spite of just having come off at least a day of being sedated, Des's eyes grew heavy.

In minutes, she was asleep.

❖

When Des's breathing evened out, Ruby's eyes opened, blank and absent.

She sat up slowly, carefully, after disengaging from Des's arms. Des grumbled and turned onto her back, limbs splayed out like a starfish. But Ruby didn't see this. She didn't see anything.

Not even as she slid out of bed and crossed the room, barefoot, to the balcony.

Once outside she approached the railing and put her hands on it, seeming to test the strength of it. Upon finding it to be sturdy, she smiled, and leaned her weight against it, looked up into the moonless, star-filled night, opened her mouth, and howled.

❖

It was night, and Ruby was running with the Moon. Chasing and being chased by it. Eternal friend and guide, it was ever above her, its cool silver light both balm and accelerant. It ignited her blood even as its coolness ran gentle, soothing fingers through her fur.

And she ran through the Forest, the place where they'd all begun, and where everybody had lived once upon a time. Branches scraped at her but didn't hold her back. Shadows gibbered and jeered at her, and she leered right back. She feared nothing.

Indeed, what was there to fear? Mere sticks and shadows?

Ruby howled her dominance, her fearlessness, just to hear it echo off the dome of the sky, and those echoes sounded like the Moon howling back its kinship and approval.

She ran and ran under that Moon. And it seemed that she ran for eons alone, and that was the way it was, the way it had to be. For she was Dyre. She was the lone wolf. The one on whose shoulders the lives of the Packs fell.

And she was always, and would always be alone.

"Ah, but even Dyres have been known to pair off, Ruby. Loneliness isn't exactly part of the job description."

Ruby glanced to her right to see another wolf keeping pace with her. He was older than she, if the silver-blond fur was anything to go by, and noticeably larger. But most importantly, his voice, that combination of scents-sounds-facial expressions-motions, was somehow familiar.

Even that loll of his tongue—a Loup-ine smile—tickled at Ruby's memory, as did the shape of the yellow-gold eyes.

"Moon Above—George?"

Another tongue loll. "The one and only." He put on a bit of speed that took him a little ways ahead of her. "And you and I need to have a little chat, my dear."

Then that extra bit of speed became a burst, and Ruby was running not with the Moon, but to keep up with her oldest friend. He led her through glen and glade, past waterfall and deadfall, beyond the rise of hills and the low suggestions of valleys, past the bare, ever-distant mountains.

"George! Slow down!" she called, breathless after such a run. George laughed and glanced back at her, a twinkle in his eyes

that she well remembered from their times studying philosophy together, when it was too cold and slippery out to walk.

"No, you keep up!" he called back, facing forward again, his large paws kicking up dust and soil and grass, far enough ahead that it didn't even blow into Ruby's face. She was falling behind.

Ruby growled, but somewhere inside her, she found the means to put on a little speed despite her windedness and the growing stitch in her side. She dug deep and found it within to run a little faster and a little faster. Then she ran a little faster than that until she was keeping pace with George, who flowed like Moon's light over the ground, seemingly without effort.

And slowly, but surely, Ruby began to pass him. Not much, at first. Just enough that it made her realize she didn't know where George was taking her. She had to glance back to see him, but he was smiling and running. Yet he was slowing down. So she slowed, too, till they were once more apace.

"George, where are we going?" she asked, finally out of breath now that she'd tempered the instinct that'd allowed her to overtake him. She trusted him, of course, but she still couldn't follow blindly. It wasn't in her nature. It wasn't for the Dyre to follow blindly or follow at all.

"I don't know," he returned happily, his run becoming a peppy trot Ruby had to force herself to take up because despite her breathlessness, she wasn't tired at all. In fact, she felt more energized than she could ever remember feeling. "That's the great thing about running with the Moon. It doesn't matter where you go—all roads, so to speak, lead to Rome. And as long as you're with Her, you can never get lost."

Ruby shook her head. "Please, George, tell me what's going on? Where are we? Why are we here?"

"Ah, the eternal questions. You don't start small, do you?" George laughed, a snickering series of yips. Then he flat out

stopped and plopped down on his rump. Ruby finally halted and trotted back to where he sat. She, too, plopped down, right next to him.

"You're not gonna be all cryptic with me, are you? Tell me that the only answers I'll find will be within?" she asked warily, and George laughed again.

"Well, truth be told and devil be shamed..."

"Ahhhh, George!"

"Where do you think you are now, if not within? And you came here, looking for answers. The Untamed, in its infinite wisdom, has decided to help you unearth those answers. That's why I'm here." George wrinkled his muzzle again, this time in a shrug. "So ask. Together, we'll explore the answers."

"But—but—" Ruby sputtered, her mind blanking now that she had an opportunity to finally put forth her million questions. "I don't even know, there're so many—"

George sighed. "But alas, our time here is not infinite. We'll get through as much as we can, but it won't be everything. So I'd suggest starting with something important."

"Lazslo Kiraly," Ruby said, the name surging up from her conscious mind like a dead raccoon from a bog. George's eyes widened and he smiled again, pained and wary.

"I knew him, briefly. Before he was the European Dyre." Nodding, George went on. "He was ambitious, smart, and very much in favor of the Old Ways of governing. As you can imagine, he and I found little on which to agree."

"I can imagine," Ruby huffed.

"When I initially went to the Old World Alphas and the preceding Dyre for ideas on how to keep the North American Packs from stagnating and fighting among each other, I was told that only adherence to the Old Ways would keep the Packs alive and in line." Now George huffed. "What those European Alphas wouldn't understand is that I'd studied the Old Ways, too,

and had tried to get the Packs to cleave to them. But they had outgrown those Ways. They were fractious and restless. Ready for something new. Ready to evolve.

"Kiraly disagreed, to say the least. Was tempted, I daresay, to Challenge my Dyrehood. But he was already so close to achieving the Dyrehood of Europe that I suppose he put North America on the back burner."

"Clearly, however, he never forgot," Ruby said.

George's smile turned grim. "Clearly not, for which I am sorry, my dear. I thought I'd have years more in which to slowly introduce the idea of a leadership role to you. To introduce the Garoul to you." He sighed, and Ruby's jaw dropped.

"You mean you were grooming me for this? You really didn't just pass your Death-right onto the nearest convenient person?"

George looked offended for a moment. "Of course I didn't! What made you think that?"

Ruby spluttered again. "Well—circumstances—and everything was so rushed and urgent and—"

"I was simply grateful I was still hale enough to pass my Death-right on to the person of my choosing. And you are the right person, Ruby." George said firmly, without hesitation.

Ruby shook her head. "But can't you see I'm not? I know practically nothing about the Garoul, or Loup politics. I've never led so much as a game of Red Rover, let alone thousands of people. I—"

"You are, as yet, largely ignorant of our ways, but temporary ignorance isn't the same as being unsuited to the office. You're learning. That takes time—time that you aren't being given, and for that I'm truly sorry. You should've had another decade or two to become ready for my Death-right." He sighed again, heavily. "I was counting on time I didn't know I'd lost. But even if I'd had all the time in the world, I wouldn't have chosen differently. You are my heir, and nothing anyone says or does will change that."

Ruby looked down at the soil and grass between her paws. "Apparently there is something that can change that, George." Ruby fetched her own deep sigh. "Kiraly wants—"

"Oh, I know what Kiraly wants," George snorted. "That dishonorable pile of fur and greed. And he won't get it. He'll never get it, and on top of that, he'll lose all that he's schemed and scammed and killed for."

Ruby blinked several times, the closest she could come to tears in this form. "But he's so strong, old and powerful, and Des will die if I accept his Challenge. But if I give him what he wants—"

"Then the only thing that dies is the honor and loyalty that bind us all, as a species." George searched Ruby's eyes. "And that is what's at stake, Ruby. If Kiraly takes North America, the rest of the Loup world won't be too far behind."

"Then we'll lose all, because Des and I can't win against him. In the end, after there's nothing left but bodies, he'll simply take what he wanted in the first place. Or what's left of it." Ruby hung her head and whined.

"Oh, child," George began gently, and then he rasped his tongue across the side of her face, once, twice, then three times. "Child, one of the many rules regarding the Right of Challenge is that the Challenged has the choice of battlegrounds and the time the Contest takes place, as long as it happens within the Moon surrounding the issuing of the Challenge."

Ruby blinked. "So you're saying I could put it off for a month, then have it anywhere I want? Even if I wanted to have it back in the States, in Lenape Landing?" So Des can die in the place she called home.

George was all smiles again. "But my child, why would you have it there, when you could have it right here?"

Ruby found herself blinking again, but for a very different reason. "I don't understand. You're saying we can do battle in a dream?"

"But this isn't just a dream, is it? It is the heart of the Untamed, the place where every Contest, no matter what goes on in the physical world, is decided, where the weak are culled from the Pack. And it is very much real. Even for those like Kiraly, who claim to hearken to the Old Ways, yet have lost touch with the Untamed and refuse to believe in it except as symbol and metaphor.

"But once here, what matters in a fight is strength of will and faith in the Untamed. For all that she acts like a skeptical hardass, Jennifer's felt the hand of the Untamed on her heart and soul. Deep down, it's as real for her as her own scent."

Frowning, another wrinkle of muzzle that felt quite different from a smile, Ruby thought it over for several minutes. "How would we get Kiraly here? And Des, for that matter?" she finally asked. "She is a hardass when it comes to 'the woo-woo stuff,' as she calls it. Harder than I ever was."

George took a deep breath and let it out with a grimace. "That, my dear Ruby, is the hard but necessary part."

❖

Des was woken out of a sound sleep by a loud, lonely yet strangely joyous sounding howl. She didn't know how long it'd been going on, but someone was knocking on the barricaded door and Ruby—

Was not in the bed.

Alarmed, Des sat up, looking around and instantly spotting her Dyre out on the balcony, leaning against the railing and keening at the Moonless sky.

"The fuck?" Des scrambled out of bed and padded to the balcony. Ruby, in her somewhat askew, frothy red sundress, didn't even seem to notice her approach. She simply kept howling. And when Des drew even with her, she could see that though open, Ruby's eyes were vacant.

The lights are on, but nobody's home, Des thought worriedly, waving her hand in front of Ruby's face. The howling continued, unabated. *Moon Above, maybe she's sleep-walking or sleep-howling.* She'd heard that waking a sleepwalker while they were in the midst of it might kill that sleepwalker. Total bullshit, but the superstition still made her a bit uncertain. Des put her hand on Ruby's arm and the howling cut off mid-note. Des pulled the unresisting woman into her arms and Ruby sagged into her with a soft, happy little sigh, eyes falling shut as Des scooped her up.

The knocking on the door, which had slackened off after the howling stopped, started up again less urgently and brought Des out of the reverie she'd been in, staring at Ruby's peaceful face. Scowling, she carried Ruby back into the room and to the bed, laying her down gently. Ruby murmured something to herself Des couldn't make out and rolled onto her side, facing the barricaded door. Des skirted the bed and stalked over to the door.

"What?" she barked.

"Is everything all right?" Evelyn's voice, worried and hesitant. "I could hear the howling clear across the compound."

"Everything's fine. I'm always making women howl. Sorry to disturb your sleep."

Des heard Evelyn sigh. "If you're certain you don't require assistance?"

"Pretty certain."

"All right. Till later, then."

Des leaned against the desk, suddenly exhausted. Despite Evelyn's parting politeness, Des knew the next person she and Ruby would be seeing would be Lazslo Kiraly, and he'd be issuing a Challenge that everyone—including, it seemed, Des—believed she'd lose.

❖

Des couldn't sleep after that. Finally noticing how grimy she felt, she took a hot shower. Unwilling to put back on her dirty clothes until she had to, Des went back out onto the balcony to air-dry. She looked up at the sky for a long time, wondering what Ruby had seen to howl so joyously about. If she'd been seeing *this* particular sky at all. Des carried that thought back to bed with her and fell asleep with her arms wound around Ruby once more.

She woke up late the next morning to kisses on her neck that felt so good, she bared her throat in complete submission. She even whined a little. When the kisses stopped, she opened her eyes to find herself staring at Ruby. Des reached up to brush still-damp curls out of her face.

"I love you," Des said softly, and Ruby smiled.

"I know."

"And I'd do anything for you. Fight for you. Even *die* for you."

"I know that, too, Des. But the problem with that is I kinda can't imagine living without you. Not that I'd have to for long if things went badly." Ruby held Des's gaze, even when Des wanted to look away.

"I'm not just saying this stuff so that you'll say stuff back, you know," Des murmured, coloring deeply enough that her face felt as if it was on fire.

Ruby smiled again. "And I'm not just 'saying stuff' back to you, Des. I *can't* imagine living without you. Of all the people I've ever loved and lost, *you're* the one I can't imagine going on without."

Des felt something in her chest tighten for a few moments before releasing with a relief that felt so wonderful, she thought she could die happily now that she'd felt it. Instead, she pulled Ruby closer and hugged her, tears rolling down her face even as she laughed.

"Sheesh, you're such a *girl*," Ruby said wryly.

Des snorted, pushing her away a little. Just enough to kiss her.

"That's enough from the peanut gallery." Des caressed Ruby's cheek, pleased beyond all reason when Ruby leaned contentedly into that touch. Then she let her fingers drift down to Ruby's throat then her collarbone, over breast and belly and finally to the soft hair where Ruby's thighs met. Ruby looked at Des trustingly, if a bit nervously.

Smiling with reassurance, Des nudged Ruby onto her back and leaned in to press a kiss, then a trail of them on and across the swell of Ruby's breast, going unknowingly to the spot she remembered Kiraly biting. The kiss she laid there was especially tender.

"Oh, *Des*," Ruby breathed, arching up off the bed slightly as Des brushed her nipple with her lips before laving it with her tongue. Ruby parted her legs at Des's touch, bending her knees. Des's fingers flirted over Ruby's labia again as her tongue danced around Ruby's nipple.

Then Ruby guided her face up and up, till they were kissing again, slow and lingering. Ruby arched up once more, moaning into the kiss as Des fingered her clit.

"Oh...oh...oh," Ruby broke the kiss to say. She squeezed her eyes shut, her body rocking, biting her lower lip. Des stole more kisses between bites and pressed her body to Ruby's side, tingles running up and down her skin, only to sink inward to her core, where molten heat was already beginning to build.

Des sat up briefly, just to see Ruby with the light sheen of sweat that had sprung up over her body, her curly hair splashed back across the pillow, the way her eyes had opened, wide but unseeing again. "You're so beautiful," Des whispered fervently, tasting and wetting her fingers. Quintessential Ruby exploded across her tongue—across her senses—and she had to taste more.

She pushed Ruby's bent legs farther apart and scooted down the bed a little, lying between them. Out of the very edge of her vision, she could see Ruby's eyes on her. Des smiled and kissed her inner thigh, and the muscles there jumped like tadpoles. Then Des kissed Ruby's vulva and labia, running her tongue along the soft, fragrant folds of skin. She used her wet fingers to hold Ruby open and kissed "I love you" onto her clit before tickling it with the tip of her tongue. Ruby squealed and squirmed and shook like an earthquake.

Des smiled and inhaled before dragging her tongue downward and pushing into Ruby, wriggling it against wet, tight walls of flesh. Her face was pressed tight against Ruby as Ruby clenched around her.

After a few minutes, Des sat back and brought her fingers, slick with Ruby's desire, into play on her clit and caught her breath while she watched Ruby moan and gasp breathlessly on the bed. She was trying to say Des's name, but wasn't able to get past "Duh...duh...duh..."

Des grinned and kissed the stutters from her lips, then kissed them some more for good measure. "You wanna know how you feel to me? On me? Around me?" Des asked, pushing her first two fingers into Ruby, who grunted and opened her eyes.

"Seriously? You want to play twenty questions now?" Ruby said, flushed all over and not just from what was being done to her. "While you're fingering me?"

Still grinning, Des leaned in to nuzzle Ruby's cheek, her next words coming out on a growl. "You feel perfect. Soft and warm, wet and willing. Moon Above, baby, you feel like mine."

"Am I? Yours?"

"Mine," Des promised, nipping at Ruby's lips and tongue. "Always. And I'm yours."

"Always, huh?"

"Yes, always."

"That's good," Ruby sighed happily as Des worked her fingers inside her, speeding up as they pressed and rubbed against a place that made Ruby's whole body sit up and take notice. "That's sooooooo good…"

In moments, she clenched tighter than ever around Des, her body going from mini-earthquake to strung tight and still. Then she let out a long, high keen that ended with, "Oh, God, Des!"

❖

"May I ask you something?"

Des kissed Ruby's shoulder, lingering there for the salty-sweetness of her skin. "Anything."

Ruby turned in Des's arms and gave her an apprehensive look, but tried to smile anyway. "I overheard part of something Julian said to Kiraly before I moved the desk so they could bring you in. He said, 'If this murdering mongrel was to go rabid again, she would still lose against you, my Dyre.'

"What did he mean by that, Des? By saying if you were to go *rabid* again?"

Des closed her eyes and sighed, rolling away from Ruby, who sat up. "Do you really want to talk about this now?" Des practically whined. "During the best afterglow of the best sex ever?"

"I think we need to. I think I need to hear this story before Kiraly poses his Challenge. I need to know. I'm asking as your Dyre."

Des opened her eyes as Ruby brushed her warm fingers across Des's face. Her features were solemn and apologetic but determined.

Turning her head slightly to kiss those fingers, Des thought for a few moments of how to tell that particular story. She needed to organize it so it all made sense. How to even begin to explain what going and being rabid felt like, and how it all began.

"It started when Holly Black Lodge Challenged her twin brother, Thom, for the Right to Rule the Black Lodge Skins— uh, that's short for Skinwalkers. Actually, it started when I met Thom and Holly during a Council meeting that Nathan dragged me to when I was eighteen. I think I was gone on Holly from the moment I saw her, and Thom and I were kindred spirits from Jump Street. Six months after meeting them, I ran off to marry Holly. That crazy, fucking fuck Tom was best man and bridesmaid all rolled into one. He kept asking if he should've worn a dress," Des snorted. "I told him with his hairy, ugly-ass legs, better for all involved that he'd worn a tux.

"Anyway, Agatha Black Lodge, Holly's great-grandmother, had passed on her Death Right to Tom when she died. That never sat right with Holly, but she supported him as his beta, even as Thom started making rash decisions and nearly going to war with other Skinwalker tribes and Packs over old stupid shit that had been settled when his great-grandmother was still young. He was erratic and all over the place on the Council. He even tried to goad Thierry LaFours into Challenging him. Of course, Thierry had none of it and pretty much ignored him. There's been semi-bad blood between The LaFourses and the Black Lodge Skins ever since.

"But I'm digressing. After Holly and I had been married for about eight months, and I was living back out west with the Skins, Holly told me she'd been having serious doubts about Thom's ability to lead and his growing instability.

"It wasn't an easy decision for her. I know it kept her up nights. Made her cry more than once. But she might have let it lie if Thom hadn't decided to take on the Couillards—you know, Clara Kitchener's Pack—over some indiscretion of Virgil Couillard's. And he not only founded the Pack four hundred years ago, but he's been dead for nearly three hundred of those years.

"Thom made a scene in the midst of a Council meeting, and Holly Challenged him right there. I remember how her voice shook, but it firmed up soon enough. And Thom thought she was joking at first. He laughed so hard, he turned bright red under that copper complexion. Then, when he realized she was serious, he answered that Challenge and demanded immediate satisfaction right there, in the Council chamber.

"I know you don't know Holly well, but she can't fight for shit, even in full Loup form. Thom'd have killed her, and I wasn't gonna let that happen. Not to my wife.

"Nathan tried to stop me from getting involved, but I was already in too deep. Too in love with her to let her get killed when I could've stopped it. Oh, I knew I likely wouldn't win against a freakin' Alpha, but I didn't wanna live in a world where Holly Black Lodge wasn't.

"So I stood up as her champion. I fought for her Right to Rule. And it was touch and motherfucking go sometimes, but I won. Long story short, I killed my closest friend to save my wife."

Des wiped at the trickle of tears that ran down her cheeks.

Ruby scrunched her face up in concern. "Oh, Des, honey—"

"I didn't really count on winning, and that's why I came out on top, or so Nathan said." Des's smile was more of a grimace. "You know what else I didn't count on? That whatever madness was swallowing Thom whole could be blood-borne. And I got a lot of his blood in my mouth. A lot of deep bites from him." Des tried to make her smile more real, but it still felt like a scarifying grimace.

"You know, it's remarkable what a truly amazing Loup can fight against and stand up to. And it turns out Thom was one of those amazing Loups, because I had no fucking idea what kind of madness he was bearing up under, how hard he fought to be the leader Agatha Black Lodge had seen in him. How he fought the madness toward the end, despite losing ground so rapidly. I had no idea, but I for damn sure found out." Des covered her face with her hands to hide the flow of tears, and instead wound up hiding sobs.

Ruby made a soft, commiserating sound and lay down next to Des once more, pulling Des into her arms. "It wasn't your fault. You were doing the right thing. Doing the best you could, at the time."

"Yeah, sure I was." Des sighed. "But that doesn't excuse the murders."

"What murders?"

"The murders I committed while I was rabid, Ruby." Des leaned back, her swollen eyes not meeting Ruby's. "The people I sent to run with the Moon before their time. It got so bad, the Black Lodge Skins couldn't cover it up anymore, and the Council of Alphas got involved. The only ones that didn't want to see me dead right off the bat were Nathan, Thierry LaFours, Beau Madrigal-Chen, Samson Dawes, and George Carnahan." Des's smile became a little more real. "George eventually talked most of the others around to his way of thinking, but he had to pull a lot of strings and exert a lot of power to do it. His reward was to be stuck with me for the last two years of his life.

"Somehow, Phil—God, poor Phil—saved my sanity. Some weird mix of magic, medicine, and therapy. It took her months to get me to the point that I could face people besides Nathan and Jake. To the point that I even wanted to. As soon as I was well enough, I ran. Away. To different places. It didn't matter where. I was running from myself, and after nearly a year of wandering, I realized I hadn't gotten at all far. That I was still the person who'd killed those poor people. Changed, yes. Cured, maybe. But still that person. And I keep waiting for a time, for a single night where I don't see their faces behind my eyelids when I go to sleep. I keep waiting, Ruby."

Ruby leaned her forehead against Des's and brushed their noses together. "Tell me. Maybe talking about it'll help."

"It won't. I don't deserve for it to."

"Tell me," Ruby said again, soft as a sigh, but with the quiet power of a command to it.

Des shook her head, but like a floodgate had been opened, the words came, anyway.

CHAPTER SIX

The knock on the door came a few hours after Des had finally fallen into a fitful sleep from talking herself hoarse. Ruby pulled the sheets up over Des and slipped out of bed carefully. She went to her closet and found yet another sundress—this one a deep, midnight blue—and pulled it on, then smoothed her hair. Thus caparisoned, she went to the door. "Yes?"

"It's Evelyn and Julian, dear. And Dyre Kiraly." Evelyn sighed. "We're here about the Challenge."

Ruby took a deep breath. George had prepared her for this and told her to expect Kiraly to make the Challenge with Julian along as Kiraly's second, and Evelyn there as witness.

Ruby didn't particularly want to see any of them. But she moved the desk anyway. Just enough for the door to open about a hand width. She peered out at the three people waiting patiently.

"If you're going to Challenge me, Challenge me. Then leave me in peace till the Contest," Ruby said quietly to Evelyn since she was the least disagreeable. Evelyn glanced at her cohorts, then back at Ruby, and she sighed. Julian huffed and Kiraly ignored them both, giving Ruby a measuring look.

Unable to help herself, Ruby met his gaze and saw nothing there but the same, patronizing, smug satisfaction she'd seen when he and Julian had dumped Des off in her room like refuse.

You cannot beat me, that look said. *Even if you fought for a thousand years, you would not win.*

Ruby almost smiled. Almost. She had an ace up her sleeve. Better than that, she had Des. No sense in tipping her hand prematurely.

But Kiraly's nostrils flared and his eyes narrowed. His words, when he spoke, were cool and disdainful.

"...in the Great Tradition that has stretched back for millennia, I hereby Challenge you to a Contest for the Right to Rule the North American Packs—a Right I fully expect to hold in trust for the child you now carry, whom I will raise as my own," he said, his smug satisfaction making a full return along with his hellish confidence. Ruby leaned against the edge of the door, one hand going unconsciously to her abdomen.

"I accept your Challenge. The time and place of my choosing are tomorrow at sunset, and the Forest Primeval, home of the Untamed Heart." Ruby let the last bit out on one steady breath.

The reactions she received were not what she expected. Instead of suspicion, refusal, or disbelief, she got confusion, blank and without any comprehension. At least from Evelyn and Julian. From Kiraly, she merely received a blink and a flicker of recognition in his eyes, but that was all she received before his mask was back up.

"Tomorrow at sunset, then," he said, as graciously as a man agreeing to meet for a casual dinner. And with that, he began to turn away, but Ruby called out his name. He paused, but did not look back.

"I want your word, and the word of you two, as well, that Des and I will be allowed to leave unhindered and unharmed should the Contest go my way."

Evelyn smiled, but that smile was a tad hurt. "But of course, darling. We would never keep you when—" She fell silent, closing her mouth on whatever ironically ridiculous statement she'd been about to utter. "You have my word."

"And mine, provided you swear to keep your rabid little murdering mongrel from killing me and my wife in revenge. Should the Contest go your way." Julian crossed his arms, his own mask cool and calm.

Ruby gritted her teeth but nodded. She hated to promise for Des, especially when there was no guarantee Des's darker instincts wouldn't drive her to do just that, but promise she would.

"I swear. But you two are banished from North America. For keeps. On pain of death."

Evelyn looked startled and horrified, but Julian merely waved a hand and took Evelyn by an elbow. "Come, my love."

"Wait! What about you, Dyre Kiraly? Your word that none of your people will attempt to harm us or stop me and Des from leaving?"

Kiraly inclined his head slightly. "You have my word. In fact, should you win this Contest, they will endeavor to get you back home, safe and sound."

"Good." Ruby frowned then shrugged. Though she trusted Kiraly as far as she could throw him, it was the best she could do. They would just have to see, wouldn't they? All of them?

"Sunset," she said once more, then shut the door.

❖

"So what's this shit about a Forest Primeval and a sunset Contest?"

Ruby nearly jumped out of her skin at the sound of Des's voice. Des was sitting up in bed, naked as the day she was born and still so unabashed about it. Her hair was a mess, all hedgehog spikes in front and to the side, and flat in the back. She looked sexily rumpled and utterly adorable. Ruby smiled and went back to the bed, sitting down on Des's side just in time for a kiss.

"Ooh, and why're you so dressed, baby?" Des cupped Ruby's breast through the material of the sundress before pulling down on the fabric with one gigantic ripping sound that startled Ruby once more. She gasped then moaned when Des's warm, calloused hand made contact with her chilled, bare skin.

"Well, we had visitors, and I wasn't going to answer the door naked." Ruby wriggled happily as Des pushed her down to the bed and strategically ripped and tore the beautiful sundress off her, hmming, and kissing and licking the exposed flesh as she did so. "But about the Forest Primeval, Des—"

"Is it going anywhere between now and sunset tomorrow?" Des looked up from her very intent exploration of Ruby's navel. Ruby stared down the length of her body with slightly dazed eyes and shook her head. Des grinned and returned to her task with gusto. "Then tell me later, alligator."

"But—"

"Later, love."

"Okay."

❖

Eventually, Des supposed she had to stop fucking Ruby into shivering, shaking, moaning incoherence for at least a few minutes. Or for however long it took to explain this Forest Primeval stuff.

But it was so hard to stop, knowing that she might well be running with the Moon before the stars were out tomorrow. When they could very well be separated forever. Bad enough that Des had wasted precious hours treating Ruby like some father confessor, blubbering out every awful thing she'd done while rabid, reliving in Technicolor every gurgle, every groan, every last, guttering gasp of every person she'd ended. Bad enough that Ruby had forgiven her. Somehow, that hurt worse than anything, even as it finally began to feel like someday, Des might finally begin to forgive herself.

But spending the rest of the time left to them talking about crazy shit that belonged back in the Stone Age of the Garoul consciousness struck Des as being both unfair and un-fucking-bearable. So Des also supposed maybe she could be forgiven her need, her hunger for Ruby, when tomorrow could bring a parting that wasn't a sweet sorrow.

"Des—Des—" Ruby finally gasped out, pushing Des's head out from between her shaking and rubbery legs. She crossed them with determination, then sat up and tucked them quickly underneath her. "Okay, we've played the Make Ruby Come Till She Can't game for the past seven hours, and it was—God, fun doesn't even come close—but we have to talk about the Contest and how you're going to win it."

Des rolled her eyes and sprawled out on the bed, on her back, her eyes closed as she thought about absolutely nothing. "Haven't you heard? According to Vegas odds, I'm set to lose. And badly."

Ruby made a rude noise and crawled up the bed and positioned herself so she was straddling Des's waist. She pinned Des's arms to the bed and looked down into her face till Des sighed and looked back.

"I had this vision last night," Ruby said quietly.

Des's eyebrows shot up. "But I don't remember seeing you at all in my dreams—" she began, and Ruby kissed her silent.

"That's because you weren't there. But George was." When Des's eyes widened, Ruby smiled, slow and a bit smug, herself. "That's right. And he told me that we should bring Kiraly to the Forest Primeval."

"Which is where, by the way?"

Ruby tapped Des on the temple then frowned a little. "Actually, more like…" She poked Des in the chest, right above her heart. "Or maybe it's both. I still don't know for sure, only that we've both been there. Or some version of it, whenever we had those visions of each other. I'm not the only one who had those visions, am I? You were here. You were in control of my body when Kiraly—"

"No," Des said quickly, quietly. "You weren't the only one."

"Then you've been there. The Forest, I mean. It can be other things too, but mostly it's the place where the Untamed Heart lives. Where all the Garoul eventually go when it's their turn to run with the Moon." Ruby's voice grew more and more excited with each and every word.

Des rolled her eyes again, ready to dismiss the notion of Loups going somewhere special when they died and running with the Moon forever and ever, amen. People only said that stuff to comfort the living. Des was even hesitant to believe in the visions she and Ruby'd had. But then she looked into Ruby's lively, hopeful dark eyes and took in the animated dance of them. She felt that painful tightening in her chest intensify, then let go with relief that Ruby was with her now in this moment. And as long as she had this moment, she shouldn't ask for more.

No, I shouldn't ask, but I'm damned sure gonna take, Des thought savagely. The last of her resistance to all the crazy shit that came with being a Loup crumbled without another thought. If she had to believe the crazy shit to hold on to the sex, the future fights, the making up, the simple conversations, and the days spent raising the child Ruby carried, then she'd damn well have to believe it.

Because all of a sudden Des realized she intended to win this thing. And if she won, at the conclusion of that Contest to end all Contests, life with the woman she loved waited for her.

Looking into Ruby's hopeful eyes, Des smiled. "Okay. Tell me all the weird woo-woo stuff George told you. And don't leave anything out."

❖

Des woke at noon on the day of the Contest to an empty bed. For a moment, she was alarmed, but a quick glance at the balcony showed Ruby outside in a yellow sundress this time, leaning against the railing as she had almost two days ago, looking up at the sunny, blameless blue sky.

Well, at least she's not howling, Des thought wryly, rolling out of bed. She strolled out onto the balcony, making noise as she went so as not to startle Ruby, and slid her arms around her waist. Ruby leaned back into her arms with a happy sigh.

"I cannot wait to tear this fucking dress off you," Des murmured against Ruby's shoulder, nipping playfully at the fabric.

Ruby laughed. "You're like a puppy that chews up shoes and clothing while her mistress is away."

"'S'at what you wanna be? My mistress?" Des squeezed Ruby tight, and Ruby moaned a little, turning in Des's arms. "Wanna control me and correct me when I've been naughty?"

Ruby's grin was slow and considering. "You *have* been quite naughty over the past two days."

"Damn right I have." Des reached down, got a handful of sunshine dress, and hiked it up and up until it was above Ruby's knees then up around her hips. "Moon above, I wish you were wearing panties so I could rip those off, too. With my teeth."

"God, when you say things like that," Ruby breathed, her eyes half-lidded and dark with desire. Then she laughed, gathering up the skirt of her sundress. She cocked an eyebrow at Des, who didn't need to be told twice. She went to her knees, laughing, too, when Ruby dropped the skirt over her head. And there in the golden gloom, listening to Ruby moan breathily above her, Des reflected that aside from the Contest, there was nowhere else she'd rather be.

Part III: The Forest Primeval

I am not bound to win, but I am bound to be true. I am not bound to succeed, but I am bound to live up to what light I have.
    —Abraham Lincoln

Chapter Seven

Just before sunset, Des finished lacing up her boots and thunked the sides of them with her fists for luck. Ruby sat on the chaise near the balcony doors, still in the yellow sundress and gold sandals, and watched Des with anxious eyes.

"And remember, as soon as I wake up, I'm gonna be all stroke-y and groggy. Maybe bleeding from my nose and ear. Help me keep my shit together, if you can, so we can get outta here before Kiraly's minions decide to take it into their heads to get some revenge. But if I slow you down, leave me. Make a run for it. Even if you have to swim to the continent." Des stood and stretched the kinks out of her spine. Ruby watched this miserably for a minute then shook her head.

"I won't leave you here—"

"You might have to," Des said simply. "It's not just yourself you have to worry about but the rest of the Packs and the baby. Just promise me you'll make a run for it without me if I slow you down."

Ruby bit her lip. "Promise you won't slow me down."

"Baby…"

"Well, they're both ridiculous promises, and I refuse to make mine if you don't make yours," Ruby said angrily. Des was about to retort with something stupid and contentious, but suddenly she smiled and sauntered over to Ruby, holding out her hands. Ruby took them without hesitation.

"Is this our first fight?" Des asked, hoping for a smile that she got almost instantly.

"This is our first case of you being a stubborn jackass."

"Ah. Well. I knew it was our first something." Des sat next to Ruby, keeping hold of one of her hands. After a few silent minutes, she kissed it. "I love you," she said.

Ruby shivered, biting back what sounded like a sob. "I know," she replied in a choked half whisper. Then she stood up, tugging Des with her. "C'mon. Let's get you on your way to the Forest."

❖

Ruby watched Des sit on the edge of the bed and tried to keep her heart from climbing any higher up in her throat.

"So this woo-woo meditation stuff George taught you better work, or I'm gonna look damned foolish when Kiraly comes here looking for blood," Des said with admirable gallows humor as she scooted up the bed and lay down. Ruby swallowed for the millionth time and forced herself to smile.

"It'll work. Even if only because the nature of the Challenge and Contest demands that it work." Ruby stood over the bed fidgeting for a few moments. "If you want, I can go out on the balcony and give you some time to yourself to—"

"Stay with me," Des interrupted to say, her eyes free of her usual sarcasm and irony. They were unguarded and so very young that Ruby wanted to cry. "At least till I'm asleep, or whatever I'll be when I'm in the Forest. Come lie down with me."

"But you need to focus and relax."

"*You* are my focus and my relaxation. You're the thing I'm fighting for. Believe me, you'll only help matters along," Des promised, holding out one hand. Ruby immediately took it and sat on the bed. She curled up at Des's side, shivering when Des kissed the crown of her head and put her arm around her.

"You smell so good, baby."

Ruby snorted. "I smell like we had sex."

"Like I said, good."

"You're impossible."

"I doubt that you'll find a more possible woman in this universe, Ms. Knudsen." Des chuckled, low and dirty and over-the-top. Ruby smiled, even though tears gathered in her eyes. She swatted Des's wandering hand away from her neckline. Des chuckled again and sighed. "Wanna sing me a song before I go under?"

"A—Des, I have a terrible voice."

"You have a beautiful voice. I hear it when you sing to Winkin' and Blinkin'."

"Well, we both know you're something of a masochist."

"Dick. C'mon. Consider it my last wish. Sorta." Des laughed, this time nervous and not mirthful at all. When Ruby made another unhappy sound, Des's laugh cut off. "You know what? Forget I said that. Let's just lay here, quiet-like, till—"

But before Des could finish speaking, Ruby was singing in a quiet, bashful voice, the words of the only song her mother had ever sung her to sleep with. Ruby's voice quavered and shook, but firmed up soon enough.

When Ruby finished singing the song about ants and rubber tree plants, she expected anything from laughter to disbelief to being gently humored. What she didn't expect was the silence that spun out for minutes afterward.

Frowning, she sat up a little to ask Des if she wanted another song, and found Des had closed her eyes, and she had a small smile on her spare mouth. Oh, Ruby thought, more tears running down her face as she leaned down and kissed her.

"I love you, too," she murmured, wishing she'd made herself say it earlier and hoping that Des heard it wherever she was.

❖

Des was running. Running with the Moon.

She ran under the dark velvet of sky and the thick canopy of the Forest, her tongue lolling in a Loupine grin. The Forest was exactly as Ruby had said it would be. And just like Ruby'd said, Des sort of knew where she was going. She had a feeling in her gut and the marrow of her bones that she was going the right direction to the place of Contest.

Des lifted her lips from her teeth in a snarling grin and ran on.

She stalked through glade and glen, over stream and through fen, and her feeling of heading toward her destiny only grew stronger and stronger. She finally saw a brighter, more open area fast approaching. It looked like a bald spot in the Forest, and someone was already waiting for her there.

Waiting to die, *Des thought.*

She slowed her run into a lope, then her lope into a jog, and finally she trotted out onto the large patch of bare ground.

The other wolf was iron gray and not too much larger than Des, which meant that while not physically too much stronger than Des, he was probably every bit as fast, maybe more so, as he was lean and built for maneuverability. His ears were pricked and his hackles raised, as he watched her draw near.

"Fascinating, is it not?" this Loup said, radiating a thrill, delight, and smug sense of certainty Des remembered very well from just a few days ago. She remembered the feel of his stubby, human paws on her—on her mate's body—and growled.

"It's fan-goddamned-tastic. Let's get this over with, capisce?"

Kiraly's tongue lolled for a moment, then he was moving faster than Des expected. Faster than she could track or dodge.

He hit her like a ton of bricks, knocking her down hard,

knocking the wind out of her. His snapping, grinning jaws immediately went for her throat.

❖

Des's body suddenly rocked as if impacted by something. Startled, Ruby sat up and scanned Des for any sign of injury. George had said the body would react to what went on with the spirit. He'd said that very real injuries could manifest themselves on her body though it was physically untouched.

Ruby watched and waited for some other sign or clue as to what was going on in the Forest. After another few torturous minutes, she got it as three long, thin gashes appeared on the right side of Des's face. Unlike other wounds, they did not immediately begin to close.

❖

Des paced around the edge of the bald spot as her challenger did the same. She watched him warily, with hot-eyed hatred. She'd only narrowly missed getting her throat ripped out, and now he'd scored another hit too close to her eyes. The claw marks burned her flesh like thin trails of fire, and blood ran into her fur.

"Perhaps," the other said casually, in the language of shrugs, yips, scents, and postures Loups had, "perhaps when I've killed you, once the child is born and the Rights passed on to him, I'll let your little mongrel bitch live. After all, she's not without a certain charm. And she certainly has quite a lot of spirit and fight. I think I'd enjoy breaking her."

Growling and frothing at the mouth, Des rushed her opponent as he'd obviously meant her to. When he faked right, she dove left on a gut feeling and wound up barreling into his body. He let out a grunt and snapped at her ear, barely biting the tip but puncturing it nonetheless. She felt a bright flash of pain and smelled her own blood, then it was done. Des ripped her ear away to turn her head and get at his eyes.

But Kiraly rolled them over, bearing down on her with all his weight while pulling his head sharply to the side. Des closed her jaws on nothing but air. Kiraly scratched at Des's eyes and muzzle, but before he could score a hit, Des gathered all her strength and bucked Kiraly off her hard. She heard him land on his back with a solid thud, and he yelped in pain.

Des rolled to her feet just as he gained his, and they squared off again. Though she didn't notice it, the foam at her mouth had become a viscous slather, and her corneas had gone crimson. She didn't notice her vision was tinged red, and she couldn't feel the pain of her injuries anymore. Even if she had noticed and known, it wouldn't have mattered. Nothing mattered except killing to keep what was hers. Never mind that Des couldn't quite remember exactly what that something was anymore.

She'd kill to keep it anyway.

She'd kill to ... keep ...

She'd kill to keep killing. The Right to Kill was hers. She'd fight for it, even die for it if necessary, and no one, no one would ever get between that Right and Des.

No one would ever stop her.

She leapt forward, snarling, and smiling.

❖

Ruby dabbed at the unhealed scratches on Des's face with a damp washcloth as unseen blows rocked Des's small, hard body. But no more scratches appeared, and Ruby was truly thankful for that. She wanted to take Des's hand and pray to the Moon Above for her well-being. For her safety. Not for the sake of the Packs, but for Ruby's sake.

What she'd said to Des that night was true. Ruby couldn't imagine living without Des. Wouldn't know how to live without her. How could she possibly rule the Packs without Des by her side for guidance and moral support? Sure, she'd have Jake and Jamie for as long as she needed them, and she appreciated their loyalty, but it wouldn't be the same.

How would Ruby raise this child without Des there to be what? Other-dad? Co-mom? Something. Oh, she knew she could count on Thierry to be in the child's life no matter what, despite whatever fragile fledgling thing had been between them not getting off the ground. Thierry was responsible. More importantly, she had a feeling that having a child would delight him and enrich his austere, lonely life. Ruby smiled and leaned down to kiss Des's nose. "But it just wouldn't be the same without you by my side, Des. So come back to me, okay? Kill that creep and come back to me."

❖

"Kill that creep and come back to me."

The Moon seemed to whisper this to Des, releasing it on the backs of beams so pure and perfect that even in her state of increasing blood-lust, Des glanced up mid-leap and felt a yearning that was entirely human in its quiet desperation.

But that yearning was quickly overwhelmed by the moment at hand. By Kiraly's stumbling dodge of her body and his fear and avoidance of her jaws. His lessening certainty couldn't cover the scent of his sudden, abject horror of being bitten by Des. That didn't stop him from head-butting Des in the ribs.

Des distantly felt the blow and knew she was in pain somewhere below the madness, but that didn't matter. Nothing did, really. Not anymore. There was only the Kill. And though this Kill was taking longer than most, Des did not doubt she would wet her fangs in the blood of her enemy. She would drink down her enemy's power to his very soul and howl her dominance under that perfect, aching silver light.

Turning with a speed born of hunger and madness, Des was on Kiraly's tail, chasing him as he ran around the bald spot, then out of it, following his own back-trail through the Forest, yelping all the way. Des laughed as she ran after him, despite the fierce, but distant ache of her bruised ribs.

"Scared little bitch!" The human part of her came forward to jeer in howls and yips that crept along the edges of sanity. "You can't run or hide from me!"

She followed after him for what seemed like miles, never minding the scrapes of branches, until Kiraly seemed to slow down. She thought that odd considering his lack of major injuries and what was chasing him.

Des slowed, too, suddenly wary. When Kiraly's run became more of a token lope, she finally stopped, sensing something was off. She sniffed the air, tongue lolling to catch the taste as well, something familiar and astringent. That was all she had time to recognize before something plowed into her from the left, knocking her off her feet and into a pine tree hard enough that she blacked out for a few moments.

❖

Ruby squeaked and sat back, startled, when Des opened her angry red eyes and focused on her in a split second. Des opened her mouth and coughed. "Hit...me...hard."

"I—I don't understa—"

"Hit me." Des croaked out, bolting up and darting forward. Ruby scrambled back on the bed till she reached the edge and nearly fell off, frightened of her lover. Des began growling at her. Ruby reached out, quick and frightened, and slapped Des in the face weakly. Des blinked, some of that crazy anger leaving her eyes. She actually looked quite amused for a moment. Then she shook her head, and some more of that rage cleared.

"Punch me in the face," she commanded. "Knock. Me. Out."

"What?" Ruby shook her head in horror. "Punch you? Des, have you gone—"

"I'm dying in there. In the Forest." Des growled, her eyes glittering with desperation. Ruby still didn't understand what was happening, but she trusted Des to know what was needed. So she took a deep breath. "Please—hit me in the—"

Before she could finish the sentence, Ruby decked her good and hard. Des fell to the bed in a heap, a trickle of blood flowing out of her broken nose.

❖

Des thrashed under the heavy Loup body on top of hers that'd suddenly pinned her upon her arrival. But the body didn't so much as move.

"You really are quite the dangerous little specimen, aren't you? For once, rumor didn't exaggerate," Julian said, laughing as he watched her with ice-blue eyes in a face surrounded by bristling blond fur. "I told the Dyre my presence here would be completely unnecessary, but I was wrong as it turns out."

"For Moon's sake, Julian, don't lecture her. Finish her off!" Kiraly panted. Julian wrinkled his muzzle in an expression of distaste. Des growled up at him, and Julian casually scratched her cheek with one quick swipe to match Kiraly's wound on the other side.

"With what weapon? I'm not getting her blood in my mouth, even in this place." Julian glanced up around them and at the Moon above. He did not seem comforted or delighted.

Kiraly sighed. "No opposable thumbs—the only drawback to this form." He shook his head. "So, we are at a standstill. She's unable to kill me, and I'm unable to kill her."

Julian sniffed in almost genteel displeasure. "So how do we break it? Maybe we could—"

But neither of them ever did find out what they could've

maybe done. For Julian suddenly disappeared as completely as if he'd never been. Muzzle pulled back from her teeth in a grin that was mostly snarl, Des got slowly to her feet, once more ignoring the intensified ache in her ribs. She limped gingerly toward Kiraly once more, swallowing a whine from the pain in her side. Kiraly's face had gone from irritation with Julian to unhappy surprise, and now he backed away at Des's approach. Now that she knew it was in him to run from a fight, Des also knew that she might only have one chance of catching him. That chance was now. Before he took to his heels again. He started to turn, gathering his speed, strength, and breath for a sprint back into the Forest.

But Des coiled and sprang at him. She felt tremendous pain as one of her broken ribs inclined inward from the coil and spring, puncturing something that felt as if it might be important. But Des was committed to the action. Even if she hadn't been in the midst of it before the pain hit, she still wouldn't have stopped.

Kiraly was going to die tonight.

❖

Ruby had been watching Des's broken nose and bruised eyes heal right before her very eyes, when Des inhaled sharply, both hands coming up to her ribs on the right side. They hovered there shaking before finally falling limply to the bed once more. Des's breathing was definitely more labored than it had been.

Ruby carefully plucked at Des's T-shirt and pulled it up over what turned out to be extravagantly bruised ribs, two of which canted noticeably inward. "Oh, fuck," Ruby said, inches from panic. She'd never seen anything like this before and had no idea how to deal with it. Des's ribs were so obviously broken, Ruby actually felt faint. As if she might pass out right there. With her luck, she'd probably wake up in the Forest Primeval with Des's corpse for company and Kiraly's satisfaction coloring the air like some vile cologne.

"I can't think like that," Ruby muttered to herself, pulling down Des's shirt. When it was time to flee this place, Ruby would carry Des if she had to, and that was all there was to it. No matter what Des said, Ruby was not leaving the woman she loved behind.

The urgent knock on the door startled Ruby. Then she was putting herself between the door and Des.

"Ruby?" Evelyn's voice came through the door, whispered and strange. "It's Evelyn. They—they cheated. Julian went into your Primeval Forest with Dyre Kiraly! I couldn't stand by and let them gang up on her. Oh, Moon above, what've I done?"

Ruby went to the door and leaned against the desk, panic rising again. "I don't know, Evelyn, what *have* you done? Are you telling me both Julian and Kiraly are in there, tag-team killing Des?"

"Yes. Well, no. Not anymore. I—I woke Julian up, you see," Evelyn trailed off miserably. "I brought smelling salts with me just in case."

Then she started weeping.

"Evelyn—"

"We have to get out of here now! If Kiraly wins, he'll kill me for what I've done. And if he loses, I don't know what his people will do despite his promise." She let out a choked back sob. "We have to go before they finish the Contest!"

Ruby glanced back at Des. She was as still and silent as the grave. "But how—?"

"Kiraly has a yacht down at the docks. The *Agnes*. All we have to do is get there, and I can get us to the mainland, but we have to go, *now*!"

Ruby had no logical reason to open the door. But nonetheless she found herself pushing the heavy writing desk to the side. "All right. You can come in," she called hesitantly.

The lock on the door clicked and Ruby backed away. She put her faith in the fact that whatever else Evelyn was, she was a Carnahan first. George's firstborn. The one who, had she been born in a different era, would've been Dyre in Ruby's stead.

That had to count for something, Ruby supposed.

The door swung inward.

❖

Kiraly was fast, no doubt about it. But even in her weakened, compromised state, Des was fast enough to catch him by the tail. He let out a high-pitched, piercing bark when she clamped her jaws on his tail in the mid-stride. Des put all her weight into her heels and sat back hard, nearly tearing Kiraly's tail off his body. He scrambled to regain his feet.

Des didn't let him. She let go of his tail and leapt on his back. Before he could even attempt to shake her off, she sank her teeth into the back of his neck and pulled.

❖

Ruby followed Evelyn's long-legged stride down halls and corridors, Des a dead weight in her arms. Evelyn kept glancing behind to make sure she was keeping up.

The corridors were remarkably empty. Evelyn had said they'd be "rather unpeopled" since Kiraly only kept a skeleton crew of servants to staff the island, and with no Full to lure them out, most of that staff would be in bed at this time of night.

"And I tied Julian and Kiraly down nice and tight. If we're in luck, no one will find them until the morning," Evelyn said, but without much hope.

Ruby frowned. "Won't they scream? Won't someone hear them?"

Evelyn smiled limply. "None of Kiraly's servants are even in this wing of the manor. And all the walls are stone, anyway, so even if someone was in the next room, they wouldn't hear anything short of Armageddon."

Thus reassured, Ruby had scooped up Des and followed an immaculately dressed and coiffured Evelyn out into the dimly lit halls.

Now, as they moved into the bowels of the house, Ruby began to finally feel as if they might just make it to the yacht, if nowhere else. That gave her a much-needed burst of energy and speed, and she was soon keeping pace with Evelyn.

The walls grew rougher and damper, the stairways more roughly hewn and narrower. There was no longer any carpeting and the floors weren't polished marble. The Old World accents, vases and lamps and such, disappeared, leaving behind only sconces with plain lamps in their place. Then Ruby began to smell salt air, a scent she'd always associated with freedom.

"We're very close," Evelyn said anxiously, pausing as they came to an intersection of tunnels. After a moment, she picked the right way and moved quickly along it, Ruby following, but glancing behind her.

"Where do the other paths lead?" Ruby asked.

"Well, the way dead ahead leads to Kiraly's helipad, I believe."

"*Helipad?*"

"And I don't know where the one on the left goes. Probably a dungeon of horrors," Evelyn said with a nervous little laugh.

"Not quite," a familiar voice said from behind them. Then the relative silence and darkness of the tunnel exploded into noise, light, and pain.

❖

"You did well, Des. Quite well. But it's time to go back now."
Des didn't look up from her gnawing. The vertebrae always

made for excellent gnawing, and she wasn't about to be distracted from that by anyone. Or anything. Not even the pain in her side. It had lessened, but it would still be something of an annoyance had she been a lesser Loup.

The body of Lazslo Kiraly had already begun to cool beneath her. Another Loup hove into her view, and she growled warningly. She had just taken a life, but that didn't mean she wouldn't take another. And for much less provocation, too.

"Oh, don't be difficult, Des. You know, deep down, that you can't stay here forever gnawing on the carcass of your kill, amazing though that kill was."

Taking one bare second from her gnawing, Des glanced up at the newcomer. Sable brown fur and obliquely slanted eyes. Neither large nor small but bigger than Des, this leanly muscular Loup was nothing special. But something made him stand out. Something both familiar and strange. Des sat up, her gnawing forgotten in favor of a mystery, and she inhaled deeply.

And suddenly, she got to her feet and paced around Kiraly's fallen body toward the other Loup. She trotted around him several times, sniffing and looking, until finally satisfied with who and what was before her.

"I'm sorry," she told him sincerely.

He gave a Loup-ine shrug. "It's not your fault," he said kindly. That made Des feel worse, despite the body of their enemy behind her. "They only killed me because of what they thought I knew. What I did know."

Des frowned. "How could they know what you knew? They hid their tracks so well."

"The laptop." He sighed at Des's confused look. "It still had Kiraly's dossier on the screen, large as life. When I answered the door, the shooter put a bullet in my head. After he saw the laptop and collected you, he put another bullet in my heart on his way out."

Des felt a sharp pang in her chest. This was another Loup

she'd failed, however unwittingly. She sank onto her belly, still ignoring her aching side, and whined. The other laughed and sank down next to her, licking her face fondly. Unnoticed by Des, a cool, damp light mist had sprung up around them.

"You've fulfilled your Geas *admirably. Ruby is still alive, for the moment, and on her way to safety with you in tow."*

"She's—how—wait, for the moment?" Des sat up, growling. "What does that mean?"

The other quirked an eyebrow, a very Hume expression on such a Loupine face. "What, indeed." He stood up again and sauntered deeper into the Forest. "I'd hurry back if I were you. Despite what Evelyn thinks, she didn't tie Julian up terribly well. He's taken a shortcut down to the jetty."

"Jetty? What—?"

"Take care of her, will you? Of course you will. You love her." He glanced back at Des, his muzzle curving upward in the melancholy smile of a Hume. "And the child, too. Tell him about me. That I may not have known him, but I loved him."

"Wait!" Des scrambled to her feet, meaning to go after him. Deeper in the gloom of the forest, she could make out another Loupine form almost exactly as large as the one leaving the small glade. Its eyes lit up green in the hard silver light of the Forest Primeval, and it winked at Des. The mist that had sprung up so quickly around her grew thicker, and Des soon lost sight of both Loups.

"Thierry! Philippe!" she called after them, stopping when she bumped muzzle-first into a prickly bush. By the time she shook it off, she saw nothing but mist and more mist. Des turned around and around, but she couldn't find her way out of it. No direction wasn't shrouded completely.

Suddenly afraid of being trapped in the Forest Primeval with no way out, Des decided to risk it. She trotted forward in the direction she remembered as being back the way she and Kiraly had come. The mist expanded until it blocked even Moon Above from her sight. Her entire world was nothing but silver light and shadows.

Finally, lost, and scared, Des stopped and took a deep, aching breath. When she let it out, she said to the mist, "Please, please, who or whatever you are that's been on our side, help me get back to her. Help me continue to protect her. Help me—"

Just then, Des heard a loud noise that nearly deafened her, and she reflexively shut her eyes. When she opened them, she was rolling across the damp, rocky ground. Her ribs were screaming like mountain cats, and her face was on fire. The rest of her was ice-cold. She heard another one of those deafening noises, and her body continued to roll limply, till she hit what felt like a wall of rock.

When the echo of that loud noise faded away, she could hear a man's voice, low and contemptuous, and smell three familiar scents. One of them was near death, the other still full of ugly life, and the third...the third was Ruby's, *and it was nearly overwhelmed by the scent of hot blood.*

Despite her still-injured body, Des immediately felt the Change flow through bones and blood, and run in prickles and tingles across her chilly skin.

❖

Des rolled out of Ruby's arms as Ruby fell to the ground clutching at the blood flowing from her side. And the pain of it was so incredible, so excruciating, that Ruby could barely feel much of anything for the moment.

She was on the verge of blacking out when the tunnel gloom exploded into noise and light again, and Ruby heard another body hit the ground. An elegant, slender hand rolled limply into Ruby's narrowed field of view, and with it came the labored breathing and breathy gasps of someone close to death and fighting with all their might against it.

"You betrayed me—betrayed the Dyre—all to save the lives of two pieces of mixed-blood gutter-trash?" Julian Prevost demanded, his voice a morass of hurt, disbelief, and hatred. "You sided with the enemy of all we hold dear. That, my dearest, carries a sentence of death."

The world exploded into light and sound once more...

Ruby, still in more pain than she'd ever known, tried to roll onto her back. She succeeded enough to see Evelyn's jerking, twitching body slowly begin to jerk less and twitch less till it wasn't jerking or twitching anymore.

"No," Ruby groaned, tears running down her face. She tried to reach out for Evelyn's hand, but couldn't make it that far. She could see her own bloody hand crawl toward Evelyn's and stop mere inches away. But it may as well have been a mile.

Then something wedged itself under her right side and rolled her fully onto her back. This time, she did black out briefly from the pain, but when she returned to herself, Julian stood over her with a gun pointed straight at her heart. His narrow, aristocratic features were pinched with anger and something that she might have called grief had he been a more humane person.

"Enjoy running in your precious Forest forever," he spat with contempt, cocking the gun, one steady finger on the trigger. Ruby closed her eyes, tears still leaking from them, preferring darkness as her last sight rather than Julian Prevost's face. She didn't see the black blur wearing Des's clothes streak over her prone body and slam, snapping muzzle first, into Julian's abdomen, snarling and growling.

She opened her eyes when the screaming started, and all she could see was the rocky ceiling. She instinctively tried to sit up, and a tsunami of pain crashed into her, knocking her back to the floor and casting darkness over her vision.

Her last thought as unbeing came for her was of the child she carried, and that she would've liked to see his face.

Chapter Eight

Des paced around Julian's nearly headless body, sniffing it, making certain it was dead. Once satisfied, she snorted out that hated scent and went over to Ruby, sparing a glance for Evelyn—also dead, with two silver bullets to the chest, one of which was a heart-shot—as she did so.

But Ruby smelled like life, life scrambling to fix itself, to repair itself. The golden sundress was bloody, and the hole from which the blood had come was still far too large and too open for Des's liking. But Des knew Ruby would survive.

What of the child, though? Des wondered, whining. *What of Thierry's child? And what of pursuit? Eventually there'll be some. We have to get out of here, first and foremost.* Des shuddered as she prepared to change back into Hume form.

A few minutes later, a shaking and sweating Des in clothing gone much askew crawled closer to Ruby and brushed her hair away from her cool, ashen face. "I'm here," Des said breathlessly, winded and tired from the Change twice in less than ten minutes. "I'm here and I love you."

Cupping Ruby's face in her hand, she leaned down to kiss her pale lips, and then she gathered the other woman into her arms. She stood carefully, a bit unsteady but resolved not to jostle or drop Ruby, and she staggered down the tunnel in the direction she suspected Ruby and Evelyn had been going before Julian intercepted them.

❖

Des emerged from the tunnel into the night air and onto a small pontoon dock, where two speedboats and a yacht were tied. The yacht had the moniker *Agnes* painted on the side in vivid crimson paint. Gazing warily at the placid, deep blue sea that stretched endlessly behind the three boats, Des understood how Evelyn had meant to escape the island.

"Ah, fuck, I can't drive one of these things, can you, babe?" Des asked the unconscious woman in her arms. Ruby didn't so much as twitch, and Des sighed. "I guess I'll have to learn quick."

Walking very carefully across the dock, scared every moment of it since she couldn't swim, Des made her way toward what had to be the world's worst escape plan. In fact, Des wasn't even sure a yacht this big could be crewed by two, let alone one.

But maybe if Des could just get them to open water, they would have a chance of rescue.

Or of getting so hopelessly lost that they starved to death on the high seas…

That's great, Jennifer…way to keep it positive, Des thought ruefully, eying the ladder leading up to the *Agnes*. "Okay, baby, I'm gonna have to put you in a fireman's carry so I can climb this ladder…it's probably gonna hurt, but there's no other way to get you up there, okay? Okay."

Switching her hold on Ruby to the aforementioned fireman's carry slowly, tentatively, Des took a breath and gripped the cool metal ladder with one hand.

❖

"Goddamn fucking bullshit manual—fucking c'mon, man! How'm I supposed to drive this shit? Moon Above!"

Ruby would've smiled but for the dull, yet intense ache in her side. Instead, she opened her eyes. She was covered in a crimson duvet and lying on what seemed to be an incredibly comfortable twin mattress on the floor of what looked like the helm of a ship, steering wheel and all.

"The *Agnes*," Ruby coughed out.

Des, who was standing at the wheel balancing a rather thick book on top of it, turned to look at her.

"Baby, you're awake!" Des closed the book and knelt next to Ruby, who mustered up a smile despite the pain in her side. "How're you feeling?"

"Like I got gut-shot, then run over," Ruby said weakly

Des smiled and kissed her gently. "Not far from the truth. You got shot."

"Again?"

"In the side. Julian," Des added apologetically.

Ruby sighed and winced at the sharp twinge it caused, remembering something else as well. "He shot Evelyn, too. She's dead, isn't she?"

Des nodded once. "But so's Julian. I made sure of that," she added grimly. "Now we just have to get outta this place. But I can't make heads nor tails of this," she said, shaking the book.

Ruby wiped the tears from her eyes. Evelyn had done a lot of wrong, but in the end, she'd tried to make it right. She'd deserved a better end than she got. Ruby took the book from Des and flipped through it.

It turned out to be a manual for the *Agnes*.

"Please tell me any of that makes sense to you?" Des asked nervously, glancing out the windows on the port side. "'Cause I've been going over it for at least an hour, and I still don't even know how to start the damn thing."

"Well, having the keys might be a good start," Ruby said.

"There might be a spare set somewhere in here. Or maybe on Evelyn's b-body."

"Spares. Right. Lemme look." With another quick kiss, Des reached into the nooks and crannies around the wheel, feeling around corners.

Ruby smiled a little and then frowned, her hand going to her abdomen. The cloth covering it was stiff with drying blood. She remembered she had more than herself and Des to worry about. *Please be okay, little one. Your father is a tough, tenacious Loup, so I know you are, too. Hold on. I'm healing as fast as I can.*

She looked at the manual, scanning the table of contents quickly. She touched on words here and there until something in particular caught her attention.

When you need to send a Mayday message...

"Des!" she called excitedly.

Des was at her side in a second, kneeling once more. "What? Didja figure out how to drive this damn boat?"

"Nope. But I did find the next best thing." She held up the book and watched the penny drop behind her lover's dark eyes.

Des kissed her all over, her lips, the tip of her nose, her eyelids. "You're so fucking smart. A fucking genius!"

"That I am. We have one problem, though."

"And what's that?"

"We still need the keys."

❖

When Des let herself back into the helm ten minutes later, she jingled the set of keys she'd taken from Evelyn's body and grinned. "For once, something was easy-peasy about this clusterfuck. They were under her body, so they musta fallen out of her pocket or something when she fell. But they were there."

Ruby grinned back weakly. "How'd you even get into the helm without the keys?"

Des snorted and strode over to the steering wheel. "I broke the lock, of course."

"Of course."

❖

By the time they got the *Agnes* moving, the New Moon-Waxing was high above them. Des moved them jerkily away from the dock, swearing all the way. Following Ruby's admonition not to hug the coastline because of rocks, Des steered them to open water. They left the Mayday broadcast running the whole time.

The island itself was far behind them when the radio sputtered to life, startling the hell out of Des and waking Ruby from a light doze. The scratchy voice issuing from the radio in what sounded like Greek was the most beautiful thing Ruby had ever heard.

Des pushed the PTT button and leaned down to talk. "Mayday. Mayday. Mayday," she began clearly and loudly, just as stated in the manual. "This is the *Agnes. Agnes. Agnes.*"

Des read the boat registration number in the back of the manual, repeated "Mayday" and "*Agnes,*" then gave the latitude and longitude of the boat from the digital readout panel. She stated the nature of their emergency and said, "Over."

Ruby closed her eyes again and dared to feel optimistic.

The staticky gabbling of the thickly accented yet English-speaking voice over the radio soon lulled her into a light but much-needed doze. Everything would be all right at last.

❖

Des and Ruby had been in a little room for hours answering questions regarding the murder of Thierry LaFours and Des's alleged kidnapping.

Des told that much-altered story to Interpol. She said nothing about Ruby's kidnapping, and neither did Ruby. Neither woman chose to explain how Ruby had gotten to Europe at all, or how she'd wound up in a bloody dress with a bullet hole, yet sustained no visible injuries.

Interpol did not seem terribly impressed.

Finally, Des got sick of the third degree and growled *"Enough!"* in a voice that'd made the detective questioning them actually step back. Then she demanded her phone call. Des held Ruby's hand through it all. Ruby had a blanket wrapped around her shoulders and squeezed Des's hand occasionally to reassure and calm her.

Interpol finally agreed to let them have their phone call.

"'Bout damn time," Des muttered, following one of the officers out into the hall. She glanced back at Ruby, who sat rather regally in her uncomfortable seat as the other officer that'd been in the room came at her from the "good cop" angle in Des's absence. Des smirked. That cop didn't know what a brick wall was, but he'd learn soon enough.

❖

Jake had finally managed to fall asleep after a sadly usual late night listening to constant updates from Thierry's people about the efforts to find both Thierry's killer and Des's kidnapper. And there was precious little to report no matter how little sleep Jake got or how much he buried himself in the intricacies of working on a disputed claim between two families of the Coulter Pack. A *land* dispute, of all things, in this century. It was all so…Hatfield vs. McCoy, and it did nothing to distract Jake's mind from the things he couldn't change. But Jake had stayed at it till long after he'd sent a nodding James off to bed.

"Don't work too late, love," James said sternly, kissing Jake's unshaven downy cheek.

Jake had smiled. "When do I ever do that?" James gave him such a harsh look, Jake laughed. "I'll be up as soon as I can, babe. Before Moonset."

Sighing in resigned dissatisfaction, James accepted that with another kiss before taking himself to bed. But Jake had indeed managed to get the compromise over the disputed land hammered out and faxed to both families before Moonset, along with a missive that implied disagreement with the compromise would not be tolerated. Then he'd shuffled off to his bedroom, anticipating cool sheets to slide under and a warm boyfriend to snuggle up to.

It was every bit as perfect as advertised. Maybe even a bit more. Jake had managed to maneuver a snoring James into his arms without waking him and was off to dreamland himself when the phone rang. His eyes popped open, gritty and burning. He looked at his clock/radio, swore, then picked up the cordless with a sigh before it could wake James.

"Coulter residence, Jacob speaking," he said less than graciously, half expecting it to be the Hatfields and McCoys with more make-work problems or some other issue that could've damned well waited another couple hours till the sun came up. But after two words, he slid out from under James, who snored on obliviously. Jake did his best not to laugh and cry all at once.

"You're alive—" Jake cut into a full-fledged, familiar, Jenny-Benny rant to say. Then he was, in fact, laughing and crying. His heart beat arhythmically and too fast in his chest. Slightly dizzy, he stumbled over to his writing desk and sat down, running a hand through his hair. "God, Jenny—"

But the grim, tired voice on the other end had gone on

about being kidnapped and finding Ruby, and Lazslo Kiraly, and Interpol and being detained in Greece—

"Wait—wait—wait, Des," Jake said. "From the beginning, please. And talk slow." He opened one of the drawers of his desk and took out a lined yellow legal pad and a pen.

By the time the call ended, the first three pages of the legal pad were filled with Jake's large scrawl, seemingly disordered, with things circled at what appeared to be random, and little drawings of wolves near certain words and names.

But at the top of the page, circled and with a little wolf next to it, were a name and a city: Nicholai Korinsky: Paris.

❖

"I hate flying," Jake said weakly. James slid an arm around his waist, easily managing the large suitcase and even larger wheeled suitcase with his right hand. "If Loups were meant to fly, the Moon Herself would've given us all jet-packs at birth."

James almost smiled as he steered them through Arrivals in Athens International. "Maybe we'll take a ship back home, hmm? How does that sound?"

"Like yet another nightmare. For Jenny-Benny, at least. She hates boats and gets motion sickness like you wouldn't believe. Her bitching alone would make the trip a nightmare for us. I'd rather risk the plane, again."

James barked a surprised laugh then stopped, pointing. "And there, unless my eyes deceive me, would be Monsieur Korinski."

Jake followed James's finger to the left. Once a milling crowd of tourists passed, he saw a man with an intense face and slicked-back black hair. He wore a tailored blue suit and held a sign that read COULTER/CARNAHAN. He scanned the arrivals intently. After a few more seconds, he saw the approaching couple. As Jake and James swerved to make their way toward him, a huge smile broke out on his solemn, focused face, and he began waving and jumping up and down excitedly.

James and Jake glanced at each other and shrugged. "Oh-kay. Ten bucks says he's queer," James murmured under his breath.

Jake snorted. "No takers."

❖

"I hate cars," Jake muttered as please-call-me-Nicolae took another sharp, scary right toward the police station. Behind them, James exclaimed, "Fuck!" and buckled his seat belt. Jake leaned his head against the passenger side window and closed his eyes. It didn't help.

"—really did intend to stay out of it, but word of Dyre Kiraly's death and his involvement in your sister's kidnapping spread so quickly that my Alpha, who plans to Contest for the vacant Dyrehood, decided to get involved on the side of the angels," Nicolae said wryly. Jake found his accent rather strange, but amusing. He spoke English with a mix of French consonants and Polish vowels.

"Well, it wasn't just my sister he kidnapped, but my Dyre as well," Jake said. "He only took my sister so she could champion Ruby in a Contest." He peeked out from under his squinched-open eyelids and into the brightly lit night whipping by. He was soon very sorry he did. "He was probably behind the Purge, which took out most of the North American Alphas as well."

"Yes, we heard about the Purge over here," Nicolae said gravely. "It was a scandal. That someone would do such a horrible, dishonorable thing. It's unthinkable."

"Yeah, except that someone did think of it. Kiraly did," James said bitterly. "And he and Julian Prevost dragged my sister into the whole mess and got her killed. No doubt the goddamn

Cleaners have already been there and the bodies disposed of, so there isn't even anything for me to bury."

Nicolae was silent for a few moments before responding. "I am so sorry for your loss, Mr. Carnahan."

James sighed. "It's not your fault, Nicolae. But thanks. And it's James or Jamie. 'Mr. Carnahan' was my grandfather."

"Eh? Oh! Ah, ha-ha!" Nicolae laughed, and the mood in the car lightened a bit.

"So, has Interpol charged my sister or Ruby with anything yet? I haven't spoken to Des since early this morning."

"No charges yet. And not likely to be, either. My Alpha's attorneys have taken their case, and the lead attorney says that certain things look bad, like the unidentified and so far unexplained blood Des and Ruby were covered in, and their story has some holes, but Interpol has no evidence to charge them with. Right now, they're just questioning them and badgering them to see if they slip up or change their story." Nicolae sighed, too. "They haven't yet been released or allowed to sleep, however."

"Uh-oh," Jake said, laughing a little as he thought on the bag of fun that was a sleep-deprived Des. "Shit just got real for those assholes." Snorting, he leaned back in his seat. After a few moments, James settled his hand on Jake's shoulder. Jake tried not to worry too much and counted the arrhythmic beats of his damaged heart instead.

❖

All told, from the moment Des and Ruby arrived at the police station, it took a total of fifty hours to get them released.

Des was given her duffel and everything that'd been in it, except for her passport. She and Ruby, each wearing a red tracksuit and tennies provided by Interpol, as their bloody clothes had been taken as evidence, were politely but firmly asked not to leave Greece for the next week. Huffing, Des grabbed the empty duffel and the large plastic bag with all her stuff and marched out of the police station, Ruby at her side.

"Well, maybe a week in Greece won't be so bad," Ruby said optimistically as she crowded into the back of the car with Des and James. "It'll be a vacation. Sort of a mandatory one, but fun! And in that time, maybe one of you knows someone who can fake me up a passport so I can go home? Maybe one that says I legally left home, too?"

"Consider it done," Nicolae said grandly, starting up the car. With near-silent groans, the other four buckled their seat belts.

❖

"No!" Ruby bolted up out of a thin sleep, breathing hard, her arms up in a defensive posture. When she realized she was awake, she relaxed somewhat, slumping her shoulders and dropping her arms to her sides. The watery first light of dawn leavened the darkness of their hotel room.

"Bad dreams?"

Ruby looked over to the small writing desk and chair where Des sat, watching her with obvious concern. She wore one of the hotel's bathrobes, and she looked like she'd been wide awake for quite a while.

Ruby blushed. "I dunno. I don't remember," she lied, looking away. "What time is it?"

"Time to get up, I suppose." Des stood and crossed to the bed, where she sat down heavily. "Baby, you've tossed and turned every night for the past four days. You wake up screaming or calling out for help, and it's getting worse."

Ruby shook her head, still refusing to meet Des's eyes. "Maybe it's just being so close to where everything happened. Maybe it'll be better once we get home."

"Maybe," Des agreed tentatively. "But what if it *doesn't* get better?"

"It will." *It has to.*

Des sighed, cupping Ruby's face in her hand. At last, Ruby looked at her, and smiled a little.

Des smiled back. "I love you," she said softly, fervently.

Ruby leaned into Des's touch. "I love you, too."

❖

They had a long but uneventful flight back home. Des slept deeply for most of it, her mouth open and snoring, even drooling a little.

Ruby, however, stayed awake for the whole flight. She'd become afraid to sleep lately, doing so only when she absolutely had to. Every time she closed her eyes, she relived that final night. And in her dreams, Des lost. Des died, and Evelyn didn't have an attack of conscience.

In her dreams, she couldn't escape Kiraly's clutches. Ever. For her, or the child she thankfully still carried according to a pregnancy test she'd been given back in Greece.

❖

"Look who's home, Topsy!"

James held up the baby in his arms and waved her right hand. Jake, holding Topsy's brother next to him, rolled his eyes. Ruby rushed through Arrivals over to the couple and the babies, already cooing and talking in baby-talk. Des came along at a more sedate pace, handling their meager luggage and glaring at fellow passengers who got in her way.

Ruby got to James first and kissed Topsy's pajamaed feet until Topsy laughed. By the time Des caught up, Ruby had moved on to the other twin—Turvy, presumably—and was doing the same thing. Des had never actually participated in kissy-feet, but she was surprised to have missed it as much as she had. And to her eyes, the twins looked way bigger than they had just eleven days ago.

They grow so fast. Like mushrooms, she thought sardonically. *Nathan's missing it. Where the hell is he? What's he doing that's more important than being here? Moon Above, Nathan, where are you?*

❖

Later that night, unable to sleep because of jet lag and not wanting to deal with nightmares, Ruby slipped out of bed, leaving behind a snoring Des, who could sleep anywhere, anytime.

She put on her bathrobe and padded out into the hallway and to the back stair, of a mind to have some ice cream. But when she got to the kitchen, she saw she wasn't the only one to have that idea.

James looked up morosely as she came in. "Hey, Ruby."

"James," she said, smiling a little. She eyed the carton of ice cream. "Is that Bing cherry vanilla?"

"Indeed it is," James said, about to dig his spoon right back in. He paused, smiling sheepishly, and pushed the carton toward her. "Feel free to grab another spoon. I swear I've had all my shots."

Laughing, Ruby did just that. She sat on the stool next to James and took a spoonful of ice cream. It tasted heavenly.

"So, we have the same taste in ice cream," she noted.

James's smile turned melancholy. "Not exactly. Bing cherry vanilla was Evvie's favorite." He sighed. "Personally, I think it's vile."

If there was anything to say to that, Ruby didn't know what it was. So she focused on the ice cream for a bit, reveling in the cold sweetness of the vanilla and the exotic taste of the cherries, which she'd always loved. While she ate, she felt James's attention on her, curious and hesitant at the same time. Finally, she looked over at him.

"She died while trying to help me and Des escape. Julian shot her for it."

James nodded. "I knew Evvie wasn't…well, she was involved in your kidnapping, obviously, but I knew she wouldn't go completely dark side. I knew she'd do the right thing, sooner or later. I'm just sorry it got her killed," he said, tears filling his eyes, obscuring their brilliant blue. He swiped them away angrily. "Fuck. If she hadn't married that fucker Julian, none of this would've happened. I never liked him, Dad never liked him, and Mother would've hated him. Why did she have to fall in love with that piece of shit?"

"The heart wants what the heart wants," Ruby said simply, reaching out and putting a comforting hand on James's arm, pleased when he didn't pull away. "But she told me something while I was there. Something I will never forget. She told me she cared about me. Whether I lived or died." Ruby smiled, though she had tears in her eyes, too. "And in the end, she was as good as her word. She tried to get me and Des out of harm's way."

"She was so brave. Braver than I ever was. And she always had the courage of her convictions." James sniffed, shaking his head. "Sometimes that got her into trouble, but mostly everyone admired her for it. Rightly so."

Ruby nodded, looking down at the countertop. Then she slid the container of ice cream to James once more. "Tell me about her. I knew her briefly and so incompletely."

James looked down at the ice cream for a long time, then took another spoonful, making a face as he ate it.

"She was firstborn, of course. Older by six and a half years, so Mother and Father doted on her. She was their pride and joy, and I should've been jealous of her, but I never was. Even though she was better than me at everything—and to boot, she wasn't a goddamned Latent—I only ever looked up to her. She was my big sister, and the only woman I ever loved besides my mother."

James sighed, taking another spoonful of ice cream and swallowing it quickly. "Simply put, I adored Evvie, and from the time I was old enough to crawl without falling flat on my face, I followed her everywhere."

❖

By the time the Full rolled around again, Ruby and Des had settled into a comfortable routine. They woke up, fooled around, ate breakfast, then went off to their respective duties. For Des, that meant sparring with the security staff or anyone who'd take her on, including James, who was damned good in a sparring match despite not being able to Change. Ruby helped Jake run not only the Coulter Pack, but the Packs in general.

They came back together for lunch, then fooling around, then back to their respective duties, then fooling around, then bed. Lather, rinse, repeat the next day.

Des welcomed the routine after the excitement of the preceding few weeks. She still worried about Ruby, however. Her nightmares hadn't gotten worse from what she could tell, but they hadn't gotten better, either. Some nights, she'd lie awake for hours watching Ruby sleep, waiting for the inevitable tossing and turning so she could wake Ruby up before whatever horrible end to the nightmare did.

On the first night of the Full, however, there would be none of that to worry about.

❖

On the first night of the Full, Des and Ruby left their clothes at the back door of the manor just before Moonrise. Hand in hand, they walked off naked toward the woods, giggling.

"And you're sure that Changing while pregnant won't hurt the baby?"

"Absolutely sure. That was one of few things Phil managed to impart to me that I was smart enough to actually remember."

"Okay," Ruby said finally. "If Phil said it was okay, then it's okay."

"A damn fine motto, if I've ever heard one," Des said, swinging their hands as they approached the small piece of forest ahead in silence.

"I love you," Ruby said, stopping a few minutes later, her eyes bright and glowing in the silver-lit air. The other woman grinned a rakish, devil-may-care-but-I-don't grin that hadn't put in an appearance in quite some time.

"I know," Des said smugly, and then she chuckled when Ruby whapped her arm lightly. "And I love you, too."

"You'd better."

Ruby leading ever so slightly, they hurried toward the woods once more, giggling again as the chill fall breeze tickled their bare skin. Shortly after they disappeared under the canopy, the giggles became two howls that rose in tandem from the ancient trees, and drifted high into the sky, to the Moon Above.

EPILOGUE

Throw me to the wolves and I'll return leading the pack.
—Unknown

Des had lined up her next shot perfectly and was just taking it when a voice startled her into scratching spectacularly.

"Hey, babe!"

Ruby slid her arms around Des's waist and Des groaned despite the huge smile on her face. She let the pool stick slide out of her hands. "Another one?"

Laughing, Ruby kissed the spot just below Des's ear. "Another one. I swear, this place has more secret passages than it has actual house."

Des laughed, too. "James warned us about that when we decided to come live here. He said we'd be finding tunnels and passageways for years to come. That that was part of the fun of Lenape Hall."

"Yeah, he also said Lenape Hall was haunted." Ruby rolled her eyes.

"Hmm," Des said noncommittally but held her peace. She still wasn't a big believer in the woo-woo stuff but saw no point in tempting the universe.

With one final squeeze, Ruby let her go and walked around the pool table to one of the many windows in the drawing room.

Ruby leaned against the high windowsill, one hand resting lightly on her just-beginning-to-show stomach, and gazed at the sun-splashed world outside while Des leaned against the pool table and gazed at her. As always, that clench-and-release feeling in her chest began right on cue. When Ruby glanced back at her, her smile turned absent and fond.

"Did you remember to pick up extra almond milk when you went to the store this morning?"

"But of course. You'll have all the almond milk you want. Almond milk coming out the wazoo."

Ruby huffed. "You know, I've never been sure what a wazoo is or where it's located. But I'm pretty sure I don't want stuff coming out of it."

Des sauntered over to Ruby, limned in bright winter sunlight streaming through the window. Ruby went willingly into her arms and Des held her close. "So."

Ruby grinned. "So?"

"Anything on the agenda for today, DyreMother?"

Ruby rolled her eyes again. "Just some more reading, and James'll be coming over later to keep me apprised of the latest developments in the Wedding Saga."

Des snorted. "What? Is the florist unable to get enough of those damned roses he likes? Or did he suddenly start to hate his current tuxedo like he did the last three? Or—"

"Bite your tongue," Ruby interrupted to say. "I still can't believe he dragged me with him to New York City to 'look at a few more tuxes.' Alarm bells should've started ringing when he took me to the airport instead of to Brockton's as usual. And between the flight and my morning sickness...ugh, I could've murdered him."

"I could've murdered him for taking my honey so far away," Des murmured, leaning up to kiss Ruby, who sighed happily. "But at least he had the sense to take Edmond with you. Edmond's kicked my ass a time or two on the sparring mat. He's a good kid."

"Kid? He's got twenty years on you!" Ruby laughed. Des shrugged and swayed them to a beat she could feel but couldn't quite hear.

"He's got a very youthful face."

"So do you, Ms. Desiderio. Makes me feel like I'm robbing the cradle every time we get horizontal."

They leaned in toward each other and kissed, still swaying till Des broke the kiss to look Ruby in the eye. "Hey, speaking of sleep-related things, you did more tossing and turning last night than you did sleeping, you know?"

Ruby looked away from Des. "Did I wake you? I'm sorry."

"Don't be sorry, baby. I just want you to be well. To not have nightmares every night."

Sighing, Ruby pulled out of her arms. "It's not every night."

"At least seven out of ten, or am I wrong?"

Another sigh as Ruby turned to look back out the window. "You're not wrong."

Des wrapped her arms around Ruby's waist, as Ruby had done not five minutes ago. She felt tense in Des's arms. "Do you at least wanna talk about them? It might help. And I'm a pretty good listener."

"You're the best listener," Ruby said tenderly. "But there's no point in both of us being miserable and sleepless at night."

"But, babe—"

"Oh, did you remember to pick up sourdough bread at the store?"

Des blinked. "Uh, that wasn't on that long-ass list you gave me."

"Really? It wasn't? I must've forgotten to add it," Ruby apologized. "I dunno where my head's at. Would you be a love and pick me up some? I've had the worst craving for it for days."

And of course, Ruby made the adorable pouting face Des couldn't say no to, even when she knew she was being railroaded away from the subject under discussion.

"For you and the bambino? Anything," Des said, putting her hand on Ruby's stomach. Then she was kneeling and kissing the still-slight curve. "My favorite gal and guy in the whole entire world get all the almond milk and sourdough bread they want."

Ruby put her hand on Des's head, scritching through her spiky hair. "You're so good to us."

"Not half as good as you are to me."

Des stood and scooped Ruby up into her arms. Ruby squawked and held on for dear life. "Why, Rhett, whatever are you doin'? Fiddle-dee-dee!"

Des grinned. "Well, I'm gonna be gone a while, so I'll need a small token of your affection to remember you by, if you know what I mean." The grin turned into a leer.

"You'll be gone half an hour at the most!" But Ruby was giggling as Des carried her out of the drawing room toward their bedroom in the east wing.

"A half hour is a long time. Especially in dog years."

"But you're not a dog."

"Eh. Same family, though." Des marched down the hall. "At any rate, it's been, like, eight whole hours since I got laid, and I'm going through some serious withdrawal."

"You're a nymphomaniac."

"Is that a complaint?"

"Hmmph, merely an observation." Ruby nuzzled Des's cheek. "Eight hours is an awfully long time."

"Even longer than a half hour," Des agreed. "Afterward, I'll run to the store and pick up your bread."

"Ooh, and some cherries—those really sweet ones—you know the ones I mean, right?"

"Yep," Des lied. She actually hated fruit and wouldn't know a sweet cherry from a sour grape. But she figured she could ask a grocer or something. In the meantime, they'd arrived at their bedroom. Ruby smiled at her in that way and unbuttoned her plaid shirt single-handedly. Des kicked the half-open door all the way open and carried her mate across the threshold with barely a pause to kick the door shut.

Ruby seemed to glow in the afternoon light, but Des still noticed the faint dark circles around her eyes and didn't miss the stifled yawn once Ruby was actually prone on the bed.

"What?" Ruby asked, when Des had done nothing but stare for nearly a minute. Des shook her head and tried on a smile.

"Nothing, just...I love you."

Ruby smiled, tired and lovely. "I love you, too."

Des kissed the words from her lips and tried not to worry too much.

❖

On the way back from the supermarket, Des stopped by Coulter Manor. She drove the SUV up the front drive in a spray of dust and gravel as the gate opened before her. She tapped her fingers on the steering wheel, waiting for the gate to swing all the way open, when something pale darted in and past the car on the passenger side, fast enough to stymie even Des's keen eyes. Whatever or whoever it was, they disappeared into the bushes at the right edge of the driveway.

Frowning, Des shut the car down and pocketed the keys. She opened the door and hopped out, twitching her switchblade from the sleeve of her denim jacket as she shut the door. Walking around to the passenger side of the car, she sniffed the air then stopped dead in her tracks when she caught a very familiar scent.

"No way," she breathed, her face breaking into a hopeful smile.

She trotted around the side of the SUV to the tall, scratchy bushes that lined the driveway. Unwilling to wade in and get scratched up, she stood at the edge of the bushes, closed her switchblade, and tucked it away very carefully and very deliberately.

"See? I'm putting it away?" she called quietly. "There's nothing to be afraid of here. You're safe. Safe."

Des sniffed again, picking up that familiar scent and the sharp edge of not-quite-fear-but-great-anxiety that colored it. The odor pushed insistently at the formerly calm water that was Des's undisturbed psyche.

"I can take you back to the house and you can eat. Get cleaned up. Get some sleep in a safe place."

Des heard a rustling in the bushes to her left, and she leaned closer in that direction. "I promise, no one here will hurt—"

The pale figure leapt out of the bushes right in front of Des— not just fast, but quiet—and barreled into her hard, knocking her to the ground. She had the wind driven out of her. The naked figure on top straddled her and got its hands around her throat. It pinned her, not quite throttling her.

She went limp in its grasp and bared what little of her throat wasn't covered in grimy hands in submission, whining. The face that hung above hers was scratched, filthy, gaunt, and exhausted, scrunched up in a snarl, revealing mossy teeth faintly brown from old blood. Lank, dark hair hung in this face, the shadows of greasy strands throwing the features it curtained into greater relief.

Dark eyes glared down into Des's. She felt its rage, unadulterated and unleavened, beating at her mind and soul and demanding access to both. It tightened the grip around her throat.

"Where've you been? It's been months—"

"They're all dead now," he said in a rough, underused voice "The ones who murdered my family…"

"No—the twins!" Des gasped out, seeing no recognition or understanding in those dead, angry eyes. But she could feel his despair cutting through the rage like a scythe through wheat. "They're not dead. Moon Above, they've...we've all missed you, Nathan."

Nathan's fingers tightened enough to cut off airflow, and Des couldn't even choke out a word. Her vision started to darken and narrow. Then she coughed in much-needed oxygen as her father took his hands from her throat. Above her, Nathan sat back on his haunches and hung his head. He panted so hard, his corded, malnourished torso heaved with the effort.

"Philomena," he sighed quietly and hopelessly, tears cutting tracks through the dirt on his gaunt face. But before Des could answer, Nathan's shoulders slumped. "They murdered her right before my eyes."

Des nodded once, swallowing around the sudden lump in her throat. "Yeah. Yes. I'm so sorry, Dad."

Nathan looked up at her, his formerly angry eyes devastated and lost. Des had to look away for a few moments. How could this specter, this Nathan finally make the rest of his way home when so much of him had gone with Phil?

"But the twins, Dad...the twins are alive." Des held his empty, despairing gaze. "They're alive."

"The children live?" Nathan asked desperately, a light that might have been hope shining out of his formerly dead eyes.

"Yes. They're alive and healthy as baby horses. They're beautiful, Dad, and they need you. So does Jake. And so do I." Des tentatively sat up on her elbows, still looking at Nathan with tears in her eyes. "Come home. At last, come home."

Nathan shook his head to one side, then he got to his feet. He appeared to consider Des for a moment then held out his hand to her, the rage and despair he'd exuded now finally eclipsed by tentative wonder and fragile hope. "Home?" he said in his husky, underused voice. "At last?"

Des nodded, smiling through her tears. "That's right," she

said, taking his hand and letting Nathan pull her up. Once she gained her feet, she kept his rough, broken-nailed hand in hers and squeezed it. "Home."

And rather than try to get this feral, easily spooked creature into the SUV, she simply kept his hand and, with surprisingly little coaxing, led him back toward the manor. Toward home.

About the Author

Rachel earned a bachelor's of fine arts in advertising, with a focus on copywriting, and is in the process of earning a second bachelor's in English, with a minor in creative writing. She's been published in *Words 57*, *The Finger*, *The Stonesthrow Review*, on *Yahoo!Voices*, and *Amative Magazine*, *Writing.com 2014 Anthology*, and the anthology *My Favorite Apocalypse* and has had two short plays—*The Big Opening* and *Messenger*—performed for stage and screen, respectively.

Rachel currently lives in New York State's Hudson Valley and has been a freelance everything, from copywriter to article writer. She's also worked in various retail and office jobs that have tried to, but haven't quite, sucked the soul out of her. Keep in the know about her future endeavors at RachelEBailey.Wix.com/TheWorks.

Books Available From Bold Strokes Books

A Class Act by Tammy Hayes. Buttoned-up college professor Dr. Margaret Parks doesn't know what she's getting herself into when she agrees to one date with her student Rory Morgan, who is fifteen years her junior. (978-1-62639-701-9)

Bitter Root by Laydin Michaels. Small town chef Adi Bergeron is hiding something, and Griffith McNaulty is going to find out what it is even if it gets her killed. (978-1-62639-656-2)

Capturing Forever by Erin Dutton. When family pulls Jacqueline and Casey back together, will the lessons learned in eight years apart be enough to mend the mistakes of the past? (978-1-62639-631-9)

Deception by VK Powell. DEA Agent Colby Vincent and Attorney Adena Weber are embroiled in a drug investigation involving homeless veterans and an attraction that could destroy them both. (978-1-62639-596-1)

Dyre: A Knight of Spirit and Shadows by Rachel E. Bailey. With the abduction of her queen, werewolf-bodyguard Des must follow the kidnappers' trail to Europe, where her queen—and a battle unlike any Des has ever waged—awaits her. (978-1-62639-664-7)

First Position by Melissa Brayden. Love and rivalry take center stage for Anastasia Mikhelson and Natalie Frederico in one of the most prestigious ballet companies in the nation. (978-1-62639-602-9)

Best Laid Plans by Jan Gayle. Nicky and Lauren are meant for each other, but Nicky's haunting past and Lauren's societal fears threaten to derail all possibilities of a relationship. (978-1-62639-658-6)

Exchange by CF Frizzell. When Shay Maguire rode into rural Montana, she never expected to meet the woman of her dreams—or to learn Mel Baker was held hostage by legal agreement to her right-wing father. (978-1-62639-679-1)

Just Enough Light by AJ Quinn. Will a serial killer's return to Colorado destroy Kellen Ryan and Dana Kingston's chance at love, or can the search-and-rescue team save themselves? (978-1-62639-685-2)

Rise of the Rain Queen by Fiona Zedde. Nyandoro is nobody's princess. She fights, curses, fornicates, and gets into as much trouble as her brothers. But the path to a throne is not always the one we expect. (978-1-62639-592-3)

Tales from Sea Glass Inn by Karis Walsh. Over the course of a year at Cannon Beach, tourists and locals alike find solace and passion at the Sea Glass Inn. (978-1-62639-643-2)

The Color of Love by Radclyffe. Black sheep Derian Winfield needs to convince literary agent Emily May to marry her to save the Winfield Agency and solve Emily's green card problem, but Derian didn't count on falling in love. (978-1-62639-716-3)

A Reluctant Enterprise by Gun Brooke. When two women grow up learning nothing but distrust, unworthiness, and abandonment, it's no wonder they are apprehensive and fearful when an overwhelming love just won't be denied. (978-1-62639-500-8)

Above the Law by Carsen Taite. Love is the last thing on Agent Dale Nelson's mind, but reporter Lindsey Ryan's investigation could change the way she sees everything—her career, her past, and her future. (978-1-62639-558-9)

Actual Stop by Kara A. McLeod. When Special Agent Ryan O'Connor's present collides abruptly with her past, shots are fired, and the course of her life is irrevocably altered. (978-1-62639-675-3)

Embracing the Dawn by Jeannie Levig. When ex-con Jinx Tanner and business executive E. J. Bastien awaken after a one-night stand to find their lives inextricably entangled, love has its work cut out for it. (978-1-62639-576-3)

Love's Redemption by Donna K. Ford. For ex-convict Rhea Daniels and ex-priest Morgan Scott, redemption lies in the thin line between right and wrong. (978-1-62639-673-9)

The Shewstone by Jane Fletcher. The prophetic Shewstone is in Eawynn's care, but unfortunately for her, Matt is coming to steal it. (978-1-62639-554-1)

Jane's World by Paige Braddock. Jane's PayBuddy account gets hacked and she inadvertently purchases a mail order bride from the Eastern Bloc. (978-1-62639-494-0)

A Touch of Temptation by Julie Blair. Recent law school graduate Kate Dawson's ordained path to the perfect life gets thrown off course when handsome butch top Chris Brent initiates her to sexual pleasure. (978-1-62639-488-9)

Beneath the Waves by Ali Vali. Kai Merlin and Vivien Palmer love the water and the secrets trapped in the depths, but if Kai gives in to her feelings, it might come at a cost to her entire realm. (978-1-62639-609-8)

Girls on Campus, edited by Sandy Lowe and Stacia Seaman. College: four years when rules are made to be broken. This collection is required reading for anyone looking to earn an A in sex ed. (978-1-62639-733-0)

Miss Match by Fiona Riley. Matchmaker Samantha Monteiro makes the impossible possible for everyone but herself. Is mysterious dancer Lucinda Moss her perfect match? (978-1-62639-574-9)

Paladins of the Storm Lord by Barbara Ann Wright. Lieutenant Cordelia Ross must choose between duty and honor when a man with godlike powers forces her soldiers to provoke an alien threat. (978-1-62639-604-3)

Capsized by Julie Cannon. What happens when a woman turns your life completely upside down? (978-1-62639-479-7)